CAN'T STOP
DESTINY

Pamela Green

ISBN 978-1-63874-771-0 (paperback)
ISBN 978-1-63903-980-7 (hardcover)
ISBN 978-1-63874-772-7 (digital)

Copyright © 2022 by Pamela Green

All rights reserved. No part of this publication may be reproduced, distributed, or transmitted in any form or by any means, including photocopying, recording, or other electronic or mechanical methods without the prior written permission of the publisher. For permission requests, solicit the publisher via the address below.

Christian Faith Publishing
832 Park Avenue
Meadville, PA 16335
www.christianfaithpublishing.com

Printed in the United States of America

I dedicate this to someone that has showed me what true love is—my heart, my Savior, Jesus Christ, who gave me the talent to write when I asked him for a computer to write. Second, I dedicate this book to my daughter Shavonna Robertson. For a year, I wanted my children to read my book. The one I thought would not read it did. When she called me one day at work and told me she read it, and it kept her up until morning, my heart was overwhelmed because I was about to lose hope.

Also to my first love and husband who showed me how to focus on my dreams, Robert Lee Green, who would never let me believe that I cannot have it all.

To the other loves of my life, hoping they will follow their hearts and know that *destiny* will happen for them—Berthel Young Jr., my oldest and the one God used to start me off; L'Oreal Alford; Danny Junior; Artdarius Lewis; Lauren Alford; Princess Robertson; and all our hearts' joy, my grandsons and granddaughters (Lorenzo Marquis Saffell-Jones, Thea Robertson, Zadaya Angel Saffell Jones, Christopher D'Angelo Ferman, Journey Iman Gibson, and our new addition, Sir Lee Robertson).

My sweet mother, Velma Lamark; my fathers who have gone to heaven, Charlie Stager and Robert Lamark; my sisters and brother; and my brother that is with my fathers. All my life I wanted them to know that love is real because God is love. And our heart is not far from our destiny!

I also want to dedicate this to my ex-husband, Danny Robertson Sr., who was patient with me when I was writing all my books when he wanted my attention. I also dedicate this to my stepmother and friend Debra Stager who always had my back.

I hope this book will bless everyone that has read it. *Trust that you can't stop destiny.* Don't try!

PROLOGUE

" If I have to remember one more thing, I will throw all these clothes out of this suitcase and forget this much-needed trip. I can't believe I'm trusting my employees to handle my affairs with my dream business just taking off. But God knows if I don't take a vacation, I won't have a business because I won't be here to have it." She laughed hysterically, falling back on the bed. She was so happy to finally be away from it all.

Elisa is a twenty-two-year-old woman, standing five eight, with medium-long hair, silky and light brown like her French mother's, with light-brown eyes and milk-chocolate skin like her father. She started her business at the age of twenty-two. She did not know it would prosper as it had. She went to college at the age of seventeen. She finished high school early, taking a placement test to be moved up early. She was driven at a young age. The second oldest of four, she saw her parents work hard to give them the life most people only dream of.

CHAPTER 1

As the alarm went off by her ear, Elisa pulled the covers back over her ear. As she lay down for a second, she jumped up. "Oh my god, my graduation is today."

Elisa jumped up, ran down the hall to her mother's room. She was already up. Her father was up also. She could smell the barbeque from the hallway.

"Give me a hug, graduate girl. I'm so proud of you!" her mother, Autumn, said.

She was five nine, a beautiful caramel-skinned lady with soft French-looking hair. She was from Florida where she met their father in her last year of high school. Soon after finishing college, she married her father and had her and her brother Stan Junior. As she was making up her bed, she looked up at Elisa.

"Momma, you know I have to get up early. Why did you let me wait for that slow time clock?" she said jokingly.

"Young lady, what's your hurry? You took that placement test to graduate early. Believe me, life isn't going nowhere. I will already miss you leaving off for college in the next two weeks."

"Well, ma'am, I have goals, and sitting here eating your good food and listening to my crazy siblings begging for my attention isn't the life I bargained for, mother dearest."

"I have your mother dearest, young lady, but I'm proud of you, though."

They both laughed, and her mother grabbed her and held her very tightly. She already had one son graduate and go off to the air force. Now her second oldest was leaving, and she was leaving earlier than she planned. But when Elisa walked in to her father's office and told them she had signed up for the placement test, and all she needed was their signature and approval, they contemplated at first, and then they remembered who they were dealing with—Elisa, the child that was selling lemonade at the age of seven, making money.

"Mommy, you're not going to make me cry yet, are you? Well, maybe you should before I mess up my makeup." She laughed, but inside, she wanted to cry.

As they both had a moment of silence, her father, who stood six two, walked in, his complexion bronze, eyes medium light brown and, at his age, still had a six-pack. Even though he had been outside in the heat and sweaty, no one could tell. He always looked good, dressed good, and all her mother's friends had a crush on him since high school, but he had been married to her mother for twenty-one years faithfully. They were married young, both twenty-one years old, having her brother at the age of twenty-two and, later, having her and the twins. He had his own engineering business he started at the age of twenty-five. This was probably where she got her drive from.

"Come here, my twin. I'm almost through with your barbecue. The steaks took longer than I planned. But your ribs are just as tender and ready for us to eat."

"Did you do the boudin yet? Hey, living in Pensacola is too close to Louisiana gouty have my booty din." They all laughed, hysterical.

Then there was an awkward silence that filled the room. Her father took her hands and pulled her to him. His eyes were watering, but he didn't dare cry in front of his favorite and only daughter.

"Elisa baby, I know I have to let you go, but I didn't plan to let my baby go so soon. I love you, and Dad is a call and prayer away."

She put her arms around her tall father, feeling protected as she had always felt since her youth. "I love you too, Dad. I'm not going far. I'm just going to Florida State like my parents," she said, hiding her tears inside.

CAN'T STOP DESTINY

"Well, young lady, let's wake the twins up," her mother said. She had the twins at the age of thirty-eight.

"Starting over must be hell, right, Momma"?

"Heaven, not hell, young lady. I love my Adam and Shawn."

Adam and Shawn were her four-year-old twins. She named them after her and her husband's first initials. They were caramel and milk chocolate, which was the only way to tell them apart. They were identical twins. They walked into the rooms of the twins who had double rooms with a restroom dividing them. Elisa walked into Adam's room, while her mother went through the bathroom to Shawn's room. Autumn loves the way her designer did their rooms. No carpet but large rugs made of cars. Of course, it was because they loved the cartoon *Cars*.

"Get up, Mr. Adam. It is big sis's big day! Get up!" Elisa said as she pulled the cover from over his head.

"I'm up, I'm up, sister!"

They couldn't say her name, so they called her sister. Adam jumped up and hugged her tight, making her fall on his bed.

"Okay, if it breaks, you can't have my room, little boy, even though you and Shawn are always trying to get in there."

"Sis, I'm a big boy. I'm taking your room," he said, looking up, almost as tall as his sister. "And Shawn can stay in his dirty room."

She laughed because for a four and a half, he was a clean freak, but Shawn was always putting his toys everywhere.

As they were talking, her mother walked in with Shawn. Adam was the chocolate one. With dimples to match, he was going to break all the little hearts. Shawn was handsome also, with milk-chocolate skin and light-brown eyes to match, like Autumn's father. Elisa and Shawn had their grandfather's eyes, but Adam and Stan Junior had their Dad's. Stan Senior has light medium-brown eyes, almost light brown but not hazel eyes. Autumn was blessed, and she knew it with such a handsome family.

"Hey! I'm hungry," Shawn said, walking in front of his mother. "Mommy, what's for breakfast?" He ran to Elisa who attempted to pick him up and give him a big kiss. "No! Sister, I'm a man. You can't kiss me like that. I told you."

9

"You a man, Shawn?" she joked.

"Yes, my girlfriend told me that yesterday."

"Yesterday, little boy, you were only four."

"Yes, I am, but I will be five in one month! I'm going to be in a big boy school with big girls and, and…" he said, stuttering. "And you better know it, sister!" He then left the room, trying to go eat.

"Mommy, what are you going to do with that one. He's four going on forty."

They both laughed and looked at Adam who was tempting to make up his bed.

"Mommy, this one is forty, and he needs to act four." They both laughed hard as they walked into the breakfast area.

Their mother had good taste, and her father had their home decorated just as she desired. The breakfast area had a table along the wall as if you were in a '50s restaurant. Behind the sitting area was a bay window with her favorite flowers of assorted brands. She loved taking care of them and talking to them. Next to the breakfast area was a large kitchen that you step down to from the breakfast area, with an island and red oak cabinets and black marble counters. There was a double-door refrigerator with ice machine that makes water and crushed ice, and to top that off, she had crystal teddy bears on top of her cabinets that she loved. The twins couldn't break them. They were too high to reach. Next to the kitchen was a huge family room with a big-screen TV in a red oak cabinet with studio seats and big burgundy leather sectional sofa to match. She did not want a formal living room. She said she wanted her family to be together, not divided. And Stan gave it all to her. His business made enough profit in the third year to give her what she wanted. And since she was a social worker, she made money also to help have all the elegance she wanted in their home. As she opened the freezer to see what to feed the boys, Shawn walked in.

"Mommy, waffles please, waffles!"

Adam ran in. "Cereal!"

"Mommy, Froot Loops, please!"

Autumn paused and looked at the boys.

"Okay, are you sure you are identical twins?" Elisa joked.

"Yes, sister," they both said at the same time.

CAN'T STOP DESTINY

Now they spook me when they do stuff like that, Elisa said to herself, sitting at the table, eating last night's leftover spaghetti. She loved leftovers.

"Okay, young men, hurry up. We have to get you dressed for my big day."

As they were all eating, Elisa walked in her room which she redesigned when she was fifteen. She loved elegant designs, so she had a tall four-poster full bed that sat ten inches off the floor. Her comforter and curtains matched in a French designer style. Since she was the first and only daughter, she had the largest room of the four children. So she was able to have a French sofa and computer area for her studies, her own phone line and internet, walk-in closet with dressers built in the closet. The closet was so big she could put a full bed and dresser in it.

Stan Junior was always jealous of her room. He stated, "If I'm the oldest, why can I only fit a twin bed in my closet space? Why do I have dressers all over my room? I might want a sofa in my room too." He would joke with his parents, but he and Elisa were so close you would think they were twins. But they were two and a half years apart.

As she sat at her computer checking her emails, she noticed an email that she thought she wouldn't get so early in the morning. It was from one her favorite teacher.

> Good morning, Ms. Elisa. I'm glad to have had you as one of my students. I encourage you to keep that drive that you have, and you will be all you set out to be. To be seventeen and accomplish so much, graduating at the top of your class doesn't take away from your many stepping-stones. I'm writing all my graduate students, and you have my number. And if the University of Florida becomes a challenge, remember I'm a prayer away.
>
> Love you,
> Mr. William Harris

PAMELA GREEN

As Elisa closed the email, she forgot that she would have to leave the one man that she was crushing on since her junior year when he became her world history class teacher. Tears formed in her eyes. She still remembered when he first walked into the classroom.

*

"Okay, students," the assistant principal said as everyone was entering into class.

As always, Elisa was looking over her homework, making sure she aced the test that they were about to take today. Everyone was talking, expecting a sub, because usually, when the principal came in, he asked the students to be on their best behavior because their teacher would be out.

"Mr. Stanford will no longer be your teacher," the principal said, getting their attention.

"What!" some of the kids said, confused, and some didn't care at all.

"Where is he going?" one of the students asked, sounding generally concerned.

"Well, he had a death in his family and had to move, so the district had to replace him with a new teacher, fresh out of college. But I want you to give him the same respect you would give any other elder."

"Fresh out of college!" one of the boys said, ready to make a joke out of it.

"Do not start, Mr. Jones, or you will be with me after school. You do understand me, right?"

"Yes, sir," he said, sitting up, trying to show he was listening.

As Mr. Harris walked in, Elisa looked like she had swallowed a ball, and all the other girls started staring just as hard.

"Good evening, all. My name is Mr. William Harris."

"As you can see"—the principal stared, just as the students did—"he doesn't look a year older than you all."

Mr. Harris smiled. "But I am older than you, guys. I just started college a little bit younger, that's all. I started fresh out of high school.

12

CAN'T STOP DESTINY

I also had two years of college behind me when I graduated from high school. But I graduated at the top of my senior class and my college class. I will be a big stepping-stone in helping you advance in your high school upbringing, meaning I've been there and done that, so I hope to be able to reach you all right where you are at."

"Man, you need to stop joking!" one of the young men said.

"You're a new student or what?"

"No, son." Mr. Harris laughed. "I'm here to teach."

"Well, Mr. Harris, I will let all the students get to know you, and if you need any assistance, you have a phone by your desk with my extension, and they know that I do not play!"

"No, he doesn't," Douglass joked, one of the class clowns.

As the principal walked out, Mr. Harris asked the students to introduce themselves. When he got to Elisa, she paused because she was still in shock on how good-looking he was. Mr. Harris was five ten, with smooth dark-chocolate skin, soft dark Indian hair that was cut perfectly. His body was slim, but you could tell he went to the gym. He had big dark eyes, and when he smiled, he had one dimple, and his smile made the average woman melt.

"Hello, my name is Elisa Martin," she said, staring and smiling at the same time.

He couldn't help but notice how beautiful she was. As he looked at her, he said in his head, *Man, it's a crime. It's a crime.* His mind spoke back, *Mr. Williams, she is your student!*

"Nice to meet you, Ms. Martin."

As the other kids finished introducing themselves, Mr. Harris asked that everyone take everything off the top of their desk for the test they were supposed to have studied for since last Monday. As he was talking, it seemed as if no one was in the room from that day on. Elisa and Mr. Harris were close, and she helped him with tutoring and anything he needed.

I can't believe I will be leaving my favorite teacher. He will be missed, she thought as she closed the email.

13

As they entered the stadium, there were five hundred graduates. She was memorizing her speech when she looked up, seeing Mr. Harris. He stared at her in a way she thought he would never look at her in all the two years she knew him. She waved back, and as they stared at one another, her friend Rhonda walked up, scaring her and making her stop looking at the most handsome man to her in the stadium.

"Hey, my friend, I see you trying to get that last glance at Mr. Milky Way."

"Milky Way is a good word for him. He will be missed," Elisa said with a stare that made her feelings for her teacher so obvious.

"You never know, my friend, what the future holds," Rhonda said, noticing him also.

"You're right, you never know," Elisa said, agreeing.

As the graduation was ending, and everyone was leaving to meet their families, she looked up and saw her best friend in the world besides Rhonda, her brother Stan Junior. Elisa screamed and jumped and held him so tight he could hardly breathe.

"Hey, you act like you miss a brother."

She held him, and she couldn't stop the tears. "I thought you were not going to make it."

"Miss my only big little sister's graduation? Even Uncle Sam can't keep me from it."

"I appreciate you for not listening to Uncle Sam, but if he comes to put you in jail, you are going by yourself."

They all laughed. Her dad was glad to see his older son. He knew he was coming, but he even made him wonder when he didn't come home before they left.

"Son, you did have me wondering, but I'm glad to see you."

He hugged his son as tight as he hugged his daughter. They had their problems, but they were close, and Stan Junior knew he could count on his dad to always have his back.

"Man, Mommy, you still look younger than your old man."

"Hey, I'm not that old yet," his father joked.

She grabbed her son around the waist. He was six three, his father six two.

CAN'T STOP DESTINY

"I miss you so much," she said, trying not to cry. "So how long are you here for, son?" She held him off, looking in his eyes, seeing her husband at his age.

"Well, Mommy, I am here for at least three weeks, and I will be able to go with you guys to take my sis to college."

"Really!" She jumped like a little girl.

Later, she was having her pictures taken with her classmates and family with the photographer that her parents paid to take all her pictures for the whole day and night. Her parents walked up to her, with Mr. Harris next to them. He looked at Elisa, trying his best not to look at her any way that he shouldn't, and she fought not to look at him the same.

"We invited Mr. Harris to your graduation dinner. I know he's your teacher, but he's only twenty-two years old. He's just two years older than your brother," his father joked, not knowing she was so uncomfortable with him being there. But she was glad he agreed.

"Please call me William, everyone, including you, Ms. Elisa. You are no longer my student. Your daughter saved me out of a lot of rough spots with my students and my work. I'm not surprised she is riding four years free."

"William, don't make me blush," she said, saying his first name, making herself blush.

"Elisa, don't be modest. You know you were my angel."

"Thanks, William." She felt comfortable saying it and loved the way it sounded coming off her lips.

At the party, as everyone was on the one-acre land behind their home, Elisa and Rhonda were upstairs getting dressed. Elisa had a sexy halter dress on that hugged every curve on her body.

"Girl, when we walk down, I know all eyes are going be on us!" Rhonda joked.

"Well, I hope only one eye be on me, and that's William's eyes."

"Hello, you forgot, Elisa. You are only seventeen!"

"Know I'm almost eighteen in five months."

"You forgot you got in our grade at the age of fifteen. You're really supposed to graduate next year."

15

PAMELA GREEN

"I know, Rhonda, but I'm mature for my age, and you know it, or you wouldn't be my best friend."

"You are right about that, girl, but you have your whole life ahead of you."

They both paused, then busted out laughing.

"Let's go party hardy."

As everyone was enjoying the music and food, her parents were watching for their baby girl to walk outside. As she walked out, her father had the DJ play her favorite jazz song by Najee. As she walked out, Stan Junior, who was next to the DJ, got on the microphone.

"I introduce the senior class of 2006, Elisa Martin and her best friend, Rhonda Anderson."

Everyone screamed. As Elisa walked out, she was so beautiful in her long white halter dress all eyes were on her, even her father's friends, but the one person who mattered that had his eyes on her was Mr. Harrison.

She walked over and hugged all her guests. When she got to Mr. Harrison, she shook his hand.

"Thank you for everything, Mr. Harrison."

"No, it's William," he said, fighting his strong attraction to his ex-student. "I tell you, Florida University will have a challenge on their hands."

"Yes, they will. I'm starting in two weeks. My goal is to finish early."

"So what is your major again? I know you told me psychologist assistant. But you young people change your minds so much."

She felt assaulted because he was just looking at her like a woman, and now he was calling her a child.

"Well, Mr. Harrison, some of us children know what they want, and we stick to it," she said as she walked off from him.

As she left him there looking confused, he looked up, and then he began to smile, for he knew they cared more than they could ever admit, at least at this time.

"Let's pin money on the graduate. Everyone has five minutes to slow dance and pin money."

CAN'T STOP DESTINY

Her father walked up, and he pinned five hundred dollars on her. Every man and boy sighed.

"Who's going to match that?" They all laughed.

As she was dancing, William was going for his wallet to come at least close to what her father had pinned on her. As the DJ said "next," he was right at her hand. Everyone laughed. Her mother looked as if to say "kind of excited, aren't you?"

"May I have this dance?"

She smiled as William pinned $450 on her.

Everyone screamed.

"Hey, I can't believe you're trying to outdo my father!"

"No, I don't think any man but your husband, the lucky guy, whoever that will be, can come close to matching your dad." As the music started, he took her in his arms, and he held her just close enough to say, "Yes, I care, but not enough to say you are mine."

He looked her in the eyes, staring in her soul. She stared back saying inside herself, *Yes, I care, and yes, I will always care.*

As the DJ, shouted "next," her brother Stan Junior kissed her on the forehead. He pinned one thousand dollars on her. Her father ran over to her.

"Hey, hey, you can't make Dad look bad!"

Everyone was screaming and laughing.

"Hey, I'm not trying to outdo you. You have done more for her over her seventeen and a half years than I could ever outdo."

They both kissed her on the cheek, and her mother walked over, then the twins grabbed her around the legs. The photographer could not stop snapping. Then Rhonda walked over, then all her classmates. They all started kissing her on the cheek and pinning money on her.

"Okay, seems like a family affair, so let's start the Harlem shelf!"

Later, everyone was enjoying the party. It was around midnight. The older crowd were enjoying each other, and the young crowd were enjoying themselves too. Elisa was sitting on a bench by the pond with her favorite ducks she had named personally. She was pondering what her next move was for heading to college. She was planning her business already. She had always been an entrepreneur even from her youth. As she was leaning with her hand in her chin, Mr. Harris walked up to her.

"Deep in thought, I see."

"Yes, sir, I am. I have so many plans I'm just trying to line them in order. So much can take me off my focus."

"Like what, I might ask?"

"Well, for one, William, men!"

"Hey, I'm a man!" he joked.

She blushed.

"Well, William, I know you are a man, but some men are not in your reach, no matter how much you want them. So since I can't have what I want, I'm going to focus my energy on my five-year goal which is to finish college in three and a half years. Just like you, I also have college hours already."

"That's good, girl. I like to hear my students being focused."

"William, if you call me a girl one more time, I will be forced to show you that I'm not a girl." She tried to walk off.

"Wait, wait, I will not have you walking off from me again. So I will help you to figure out what you want to know."

"And what is that?" she asked, blushing nervously.

"Yes, I'm very attracted to you, Ms. Elisa. But we both had known this since I walked in your world history class two years ago. But we also know I will be hung if I approach you in any way. So can I ask this of you? Elisa, when you finish college, look up an old man, and if you aren't taken by those young college studs," he said, showing that one dimple that drove every student and woman crazy. "Will you give me a chance to show you just how much I'm attracted to you? I will be twenty-six years old."

"Yes, William, that's a date!"

She leaned over and kissed him softly on his chin, wanting to kiss him in the mouth but dared not get the one man she loved in trouble.

The day for her departure arrived. As everyone was sitting in the living area, Elisa was preparing to get her things together for college. Tallahassee isn't far, but it seemed far enough. College life—will it be all she envisioned it to be? Studying, learning, focusing was never

CAN'T STOP DESTINY

a problem for her, but who knew the attachments with it all? *Will I join a sorority? Will it help my future goals, or will it hurt me? Should I get a job even though my family is well-off? Is it time that I help their load and give my parents a break? Or should I just focus on my studies? Being a doctor is a lot of studying.* As she fell back in her bed thinking, her mother walked in.

"Young lady, you need to be ready in fifteen minutes. The plane will be leaving in two hours, and I hate running. Not good for the young back."

Her mother laughed, and she laughed too, wanting to cry at the same time.

"Are you okay, baby? You need not to worry about your future, and yours is now in God's hands anyway. You have always planned and driven yourself for your dreams and desires. I often wondered where you get this drive from. But I knew, besides being like me and your father, especially your father"—she smiled—"God must be putting something in you for his glory because it is God who gives us the wisdom and the power to get wealth. But Mommy wants you to know, out of all our getting, we were not aiming for money. We really wanted to bless others and make a difference. The money just came with it as a blessing, for working hard and blessing others and not just us. Elisa, are you listening?"

"Yes, ma'am. I was thinking as you were speaking, realizing that you raised me to fear God, and he will help me with the decisions I'm pondering. Thanks, Mom. God sent you in here to help me. I really appreciate you and Dad and Stan Junior. You have always had my back. I will be ready shortly."

She sat up and grabbed her mother around the neck and kissed her in the mouth to say "I really love you." Her mother smiled, with a teardrop falling. She was always proud of Elisa, but even more today. Knowing that she still had a relationship with her daughter blessed her.

As they entered the plane, Elisa and Stan Junior sat together while their parents sat together. He looked at his little sister, and she looked at him with that look that says "I need to tell you something."

"Okay, what is it? You know I know that look."

PAMELA GREEN

"Well, you…well I…" she stuttered, not knowing where to start.

"Girl, spit it out. I know it has something to do with a knucklehead. You're too smart to need me for anything else."

"This is true," she joked.

"Well, it's like this. You know I have guy friends, but what you don't know and you've been trying to get an answer out of me for the last two years is why I don't have a one and only true love?"

"Yeah!"

"Why, sis, you are beautiful, and if I can say so, you're not bad to look at by the body, not that I'm into that sort of thing." He laughed loudly, making his parents turn around.

They were riding coach, and those uppity people were looking also, so it made their parents look at them like "Okay, do not embarrass us."

"Okay, let me tell you because you are getting me in trouble like you did when we were young."

"Young, Elisa. You're still young. I'm twenty. You forgot, in seven months, I will be legal to get stoned! Hey, Uncle Sam doesn't run everything. He just pays me like he does."

"Stan!" she screamed, making her mother want to get up with that look she gave them. "Stan, you are getting me in trouble," she whispered. "Okay, listen. I've fallen for an older man. I've liked him for two years now, but since he is older, I haven't allowed my feelings to explore."

"Older! What older man has been pushing up on you. I will beat him with my gun. I did bring it, you know. Okay, in old, what age are you talking about? I might be overreacting a little."

"Hum, he is twenty-two to my seventeen and a half."

"Twenty-two! He is too old for you. I'm twenty. He's too old for me!" he joked.

"I realize this, and believe me, he has never gone over the boundaries. Neither have I. But it is so obvious how we feel about one another. I have decided to stay focused on my dreams and goals. That way, I won't be missing something I can never have."

20

CAN'T STOP DESTINY

"Man, you sound pitiful. But, little sis, I really think you need to let it go, at least until you have had time to date other men your age. You barely go on dates. Since you broke up with Troy, you haven't been serious about anyone. And that's been since your sophomore year. That's a long time to stay single, girl. I'm surprised you let Troy take you to your prom."

"Which was not all that. He still was trying to push up on me, and I didn't tell you. He thought I was going to let him break me out a virgin. No, sir, that is for my husband, whoever that is!"

"Well, good for you, young lady. There is time for all of that. Don't get me wrong. It is sweet to the taste. But you deserve the best, Elisa. Take your time."

"I will, besides, since that time I told you about when we almost did it at his uncle's house, I've been praying a lot for strength to wait."

Her brother kissed her on the forehead. Outside of Rhonda, she told her brother everything. All they had growing up was each other. She could still remember when he told her about his first time. And she never told her parents even though they know now, but they didn't find it out from her. He told them years later.

As they arrived at the airport, her father had rented a Bentley to escort them around Tallahassee, Florida. As the driver drove up in a dark-blue Rolls Royce with peanut-butter seats, all eyes were on them.

"Okay, honey, I know we can afford it, but isn't it a little flashy just to be going on a college campus?"

"Only the best for my only daughter," her father, Stan Senior, joked.

"Hey, I didn't get this when you took me to Uncle Sam!"

"No, I didn't, but you're a man, and it's a gentleman thing to do for a lady. I had to keep you tough dealing with the enemy and all. I needed you to be ready for the woods, mosquitos, snakes, the—"

"Hey, hey," his wife interrupted him. "Enough about the snakes. You know I hate to even hear about the animals."

They all laughed as her father walked out to open the door for Elisa; Stan Junior opened the door for his mother. As they drove

21

up to the campus, they took care of all she needed to get into her dormitory.

"Well, young lady, I know you plan to stay on campus one year and then get an apartment. By then, I should be bringing your car. You know we're a call away."

They all hugged her and kissed her bye as they left for the hotel before leaving in the morning.

As her brother was hugging her, he whispered in her ear, "Hey, only God knows the future. Stay prayed up and focus. You never know. He might send your prince charming back to you."

She hugged him tight. He always knew exactly what she need to hear.

"Kiss the twins for me, Mommy, and don't let them be going in my room. They will try you know."

CHAPTER 2

Three years had passed, and Elisa was now twenty years old. She was living off campus, working part time in a doctor's office. Learning all she needed to be a psychologist, she set her mind about being an assistant. Owning her own practice, she needed the full package of being a doctor. As she was getting in her car to leave work, she suddenly realized that she had forgotten her purse.

Okay, with this briefcase and my school books, I completely forgot my purse. Can't get into a car without keys, she joked to herself.

As she went back on the elevator, she paused as she saw Troy walking into the building. She hit the elevator door to stop it and yelled at him.

"Hi, Troy. Is that you? What are you are doing in Tallahassee, Florida?"

"Looking for an old friend. He works in this building, and I've been getting lost all day trying to find his beach house."

"Well, what floor are you are going on?"

"The eighth floor," he said.

"Well, get in. I'm going to the ninth floor again. I left my purse and my car keys."

"I see why you left them. You are loaded down, girl. Let me help you. I can call my friend to come down."

As she got her purse, and he walked her to the car, she couldn't help but remember how close they used to be, how she thought they would be forever, but fate said no.

<hr/>

"Hey, Troy. Man, it is hot out here. If you wanted to play sports, why didn't you pick a sport that would be in a cooler season and inside?" his friend Rodger said, sweating, trying to support his best friend.

As he was complaining, the referee shouted, "Strike three. You're out!"

"Hey, he's cheating. He didn't touch him!"

Troy shouted over Rodger as he was talking in his ear. Troy loved playing baseball, and Rodger only joined to keep up with him. They had been friends since elementary. They lived just across the street from one another. To top that off, their parents had been friends all their lives. So they pretty much knew everything about one another.

Troy stood five eleven, with smooth dark-chocolate skin. He had small baby eyes which changed colors since his father was Black, and his mother was Asian. But because his father's parents both were of dark complexion, he came out with dark complexion. But he was always teased by his friends, and everyone called him vanilla because he was with mixed parents. He was popular in school and on the baseball team and track team.

Rodger was just the opposite. He had light complexion, with dimples on both cheeks which, even when he barely smiled, went into his face, so everyone called him Dimples. He had hazel eyes that were big and small, meaning they were long and wide. Girls were crazy about them both.

"Man, I tell you, if we lose this game, I will eat the ref for dinner," Troy said, wiping off his sweat with his hat.

"Man, I feel you because I'm not trying to have honeys calling us losers!" Rodger said, frowning.

"Man, that's all you think about, women, women. Man, I'm worrying about my scholarship. I have three years to prove myself,

CAN'T STOP DESTINY

and I plan on taking a free ride in college. I saw what my parents went through with all my big sisters when they went to college. I'm not going through that. You feel me?"

"Yeah, man, I feel you. But, um, what about those honeys coming this way?"

They both looked up at the bleachers to see Elisa and her friends walking past them. Troy stopped and forgot all about the game. As he looked at her, she gave him a light smile as her friends were screaming and hitting one another, whispering about how popular he is.

"Elisa, do you know who that is?" Rhonda said, almost out of breath from melting inside.

"Well, he's a guy that goes to our school obviously," Elisa said, making a joke out of how her friends were acting. "Believe me, girls, he is a hoity, but you know what we are too."

"Okay, Ms. Hoity. Well, I want that on my plate tonight," one of the girls said aloud so he could hear.

"Well, I did not come here to be melting over Mr. Captain America. I came looking for my big-headed brother who decided to play this hot sport, knowing full well that he should be playing some inside sport that is not murder on my hair."

"On your hair? Girl, your hair doesn't even look bad ever!" Rhonda said as she pulled at it.

"Come on, girl, let's sit right behind him. If your brother is on this team, he must be over here sooner or later."

"Hey, sis," he kept screaming from the field. "Hey, sis!"

"Hi." She waved over and over, letting him know she was there to support her big brother at his sport of choice.

As he hit the ball, Troy wanted to watch him and her. He couldn't keep his eyes off her. As he ran around and slid into the home base, the ref shouted, "Safe!"

Elisa jumped. Her friends jumped, and Troy who was crazy about the sports and team captain just couldn't stop staring at Elisa, and she looked back at him as if to say "yes, I'm attracted to you too."

As the game was over, she and her friends were standing, waiting for her brother whom Elisa and Rhonda would be riding home with.

"Elisa, you have to introduce me to your brother," one of the girls, her name was Samantha, asked.

"Sam, you already met my brother at my home several times."

"Yes, I did, but you didn't intro. Introduce me. You know what I mean?" she said, blushing as he was walking up to meet Elisa.

"Hey, sis, I'm so glad you came. Hello, ladies," he said in his soft, yet hard voice.

"Well, Rhonda and I are ready to go when you are, little bro," she joked.

"Little, last I check, I'm the one two and half year's older, little sis."

"Okay, okay. You know what, let's just go, Stan. I'm starving, and Mother is cooking enchiladas tonight, at least that's what it smelled like last time I smelled."

"Let me go clean up." Stan threw her the keys to his Porsche. He helped his father pay down when he got it in his tenth grade. So with his good looks and charm, he drove a Porsche which, by the way, was the reason he had already signed up for the air force.

"If I put down on it, you have to pay one-third of the bill," his father told him.

So he joined the service and got a job working at his father's business. His father was not happy about it a bit. He wanted him to work side by side with him in his business. But Stan Junior, like his parents, had a master plan, and so far, so good.

"You know what, if my brother was a senior, I would have all those hot ties numbers," Rhonda joked. "Can you get him to hook us up?"

"Rhonda, you know Stan is not going to hook me up with none of his friends. If he catches them looking at me cross-eyed, he wants to kill them already!"

The girls were hanging around Stan's car, listening to the music. As Stan closed his locker, Troy was standing behind the door, waiting for him to close it.

"Hey, Stan. Man, what's up?"

"What's up, Vanilla man?"

"Man, I really need to ask you a huge favor."

"Hey, anything for our captain. Man, what's up?"

CAN'T STOP DESTINY

"Well, it's like this. I saw this beautiful young lady, and I really want to get to know her, but I was told she was your sister."

Stan just paused and looked at him. He didn't take to guys he knew trying to talk to his sister.

"Well, it's like this, Vanilla, Troy. Man, that's my baby sister, and I don't want to be responsible for killing one of my friends. You understand me? Man, you know I know you guys, and you guys know me too. Would you let me talk to your older sisters really? Not that I'm bad on the taste," he joked, trying to change the subject.

Troy looked at him, not laughing and looking desperate.

"Man, Stan, I'm so serious. I've never felt like this before. Please, man, just trust me with her. If I hurt her, I will give you my behind myself to kick!"

"Troy man, she is special, man. She is my only sister."

"Man, you know I know how you feel, even though my sisters are older. I feel just like you. I'm just the only boy."

"Baby boy," Stan said, joking. "Let me go talk to her. If she's okay with it, I'll bring her over to Johnny's house. Aren't we all hooking up over there tonight?"

"Man! You would do that for me, man? That's why you're my little cocaptain."

"Little man, you forgot I'm the senior little junior."

"Yah, yah. Just see you very, very, very, soon, right, bro?"

Stan just looked at him as if to say "I don't know, man. Don't make me regret this."

As Stan walked up to the car, the girls were jamming Maxwell on his stereo in the Porsche. Everybody was around his car. Even though the Porsche was a 1998, and it was 2003, it still was an eye-catcher.

"Hey, sis, I need to talk to you." He pulled her away while everyone was still hanging around the car. "Okay, sis, I know someone that wants to get to know you a little better, and yes, he's one of my friends. I told him I would take you to our hangout tonight if you want to meet him. And it's not a favor to me if you say no 'I will be perfectly happy.' You know how I am about you, sis." Stan smiled that look that's saying "just don't tempt me to hurt one of these guys, sis."

"Who is it, Stanley?" That's what she would call him when she was trying to keep him calm.

"Well, it's him."

"Just say it, will you, today!"

"It's Troy, our captain."

Elisa paused and blushed inside because he was definitely a catch. But he was a junior, and she was a freshman.

"Okay," she said, not hesitating.

"Really! Why, Elisa?"

"Why not? He is a catch and a half, and I noticed him checking me out earlier, but I thought he was going to cop out, knowing you and all."

Stan looked disappointed. "Let's go," he said as they walked to his car.

"Let's go where?" Rhonda retorted, trying to tag along.

"Should I drop you home, Rhonda?" Stan asked, still trying to grasp the whole thing.

"No, Stan, I want to go!"

"Rhonda, you don't even know where we're going. Call your mother and tell her you will be hanging with Elisa and me tonight."

"Yes, I sure will!" she said excitedly, like a little elementary girl riding to the candy factory. As Stan was putting gas in the car, she couldn't wait to ask where they were going. When Stan got out of the car, the girls screamed.

"Troy wants to meet me," Elisa said, screaming.

"Really? What, how, when?"

"He asked Stan to introduce me."

"So that explains Stan's reaction earlier and now. You know how he is about you. I'm surprised he lets you out the house."

"Well, I'm not a baby. I'm about to be a sophomore. He needs to let it go," Elisa joked like she really meant it, but they were both overprotective of each other, probably because it was just the two of them for a while before the twins.

"I will be on my best behavior. Yikes, I don't think so. Brother will be all right. What he doesn't know won't hurt him."

"Ooh, you, slut!"

CAN'T STOP DESTINY

"Yep, call me Ms. Slut. You know I'm just joking! He has to put that big ring on my finger in front of five hundred of our guests."

"Girl, you are so crazy."

They both got quiet as Stan got into the car. He was on the cell phone, smiling now, which made her feel a lot better.

"So, baby, I'll be by there as soon as I take my little sister somewhere."

He hung up, blushing.

"Okay, who is that, big brother. It better be Barbara, young man." Barbara was his girlfriend he just hooked up with. How long? Probably not long. He never stayed with them more than one, two months tops.

"Well, you know how I roll."

"Meaning it's another groupie."

"Little sis, you know it's not a part of the plan. Distractions are not part of the plan. Your sister-in-law is coming in the future."

They walked in to Johnny's house. The music was booming, guys everywhere in the yard, in the living room, in the kitchen, going up and down the stairs. As they walked into the house, all eyes were on them. The girls could not stop looking at all the hunks in there everywhere. They seem to be the only girls there.

"Elisa, do you see what I see? We have died and went to sportsman paradise!" Rhonda joked.

"Come, sis, let me find Mr. Romeo so I can catch up with the fellows. I got me a cutie waiting for me, and her name isn't Barbara."

"You know what, I knew it!" Elisa joked. "Stan Junior"—she yelled like a mother—"what'll you guys be doing here?"

"We all meet at different guys' homes, play cards, dominoes, pool, whatever is happening. It's like a getaway from it all. We are always around girls and fans. This is our downtime."

"So why did you bring me here of all places?"

"Because Romeo, sorry, Troy asked me to, and don't forget, if he crosses the line, hit my cell phone. I'm not joking!"

"Okay, okay, I will. Don't I tell you everything?"

"Yes," he said, kissing her on the forehead.

Elisa stood there as her brother was running his mouth, and Rhonda was talking to couple of the guys. Troy walked in from the back entrance, full of nerves and just looking at her before he would approach her. He had never been nervous to meet anyone, especially a girl.

"Hello, Elisa," he said in way that would make any young lady melt.

"Hi, Troy it is, right?"

"Yes, I see your brother did not put bad words on me," he joked.

"No, he was too busy trying to get a hookup himself." She smiled, making Troy want to melt.

"Hum, not to sound obvious, but has anyone told you how beautiful you are lately?"

"Not since a few seconds ago, or was it this morning? No, no it was all day!" she joked.

"So I have a comedian on my hands. It's okay. You can do that, love."

"So I'm love, am I? You know I might be a cute psycho. You never know." She smiled, realizing he made her just as nervous, thinking to herself, *Do I sound lame?*

"No, you don't," he said, as if he was reading her mind. "You don't seem like you are a psycho."

They both just stared at each other, and the room seemed silent, like it was just them two in it. He grabbed her hand and walked her outside in the back where it was a little quieter. As he wiped the bench seat to make it comfortable for her, she stood blushing. She liked the shivers already.

"Have a seat, my queen. Your throne awaits you."

"Okay, thanks, my king. It is well cleaned."

"Well, only the best for the best, my queen."

"You are trying a little too hard, aren't you? Or are you nervous as I am?"

"Yes, I am. We go to the same school, and I never see you, Elisa. Where have you been? And please tell me you are not with another dude?"

CAN'T STOP DESTINY

"Well, no. It's just that I'm into my studies, and my after-school job keeps me so busy. I don't have time much for a boyfriend. I'm saving for my future business I plan on having before I'm twenty-six."

"Before you're twenty-six! What's the hurry? You got five to six years tops to worry about that type of stuff."

"Well, my father started his business at the age of twenty-five, and he gave my brother and me a good life. And I want the same for my kids."

"So we are having kids, aren't we?" He laughed and blushed at the same time.

"No, no, I mean…" she said quickly, not wanting to sound like desperately wanting to be housewife.

"I really understand. I like that you have goals and that you want a family one day."

"Yes, I do, in the late future, one day. I have to finish college first. I'm planning on going to Florida State University."

"Hey, girl you got your plans together, don't you? So you'll be in the state capital?"

"Yes."

"Why there?" Troy asked, being very interested. He had never had girls talk about their future the way she did.

"Well, I plan on going to school for psychology, and I will be starting my own mental therapy clinic for families with mental issues. I care about people who feel helpless, and I want to help God heal their fears."

Troy just stared at her. She seemed even more beautiful to him just listening to her talk.

"I'm sorry, I'm just going on and on," Elisa said, blushing.

"No, you are really blessing me with your conversation. You are making me feel embarrassed though. I have plans also, but I'm focusing on a scholarship in either track or baseball. I haven't even thought about what kind of business I want or a family. Well, that's never been a thought. I know I want that one day. Most people do, right?"

"Well, to tell you the truth, I haven't heard Stan Junior say anything about it. He only talks about Stan."

"So you always go to his games?"

"No, but I do try to make a couple of them. I'm working in the hospital after school with my mother. She is a social worker at West Florida Hospital. I guess that's where I get my desire from. Once when I was in my mother's office when I was around twelve or thirteen, I saw my mother helping a patient. The mother had a mental problem, and the husband and kids seemed so helpless. They just wanted her healed. I ran to my mother's bathroom. I cried, and I decided that day I would not let another person hurt and not try to help."

"Man, girl, that is so amazing! I'm hurting just listening the way you say it."

She stood and walked off, thinking about all she was feeling at that moment. He walked over to her and gently turned her around, putting his hands on her chin, and lifted her face. He pulled her close to him with his other hand. He went in softly and kissed her. He felt like she belonged where she was, in his arms. She gave in gently, and the kiss was everything she hoped for. As he stopped, they noticed the crowd had started leaving.

"Well, I didn't mean to kiss you like that. I just, I…" He was speechless.

"I didn't mind. It was actually good." She laughed.

"Hey, there you go," Stan said, looking curious.

"Hi, bro," she said, feeling lighter than normal.

"You ready, sis? I have a hot date, and Troy was a gentleman around my sister, I hope?"

"Yes, sir. Can I have your number, Elisa?" he asked nervously.

"Yes, walk me out, will you? I will save it in your phone. Don't worry. I have my own line in my room, and I'll give you my cell number too."

"Hey, you two are a little too friendly for me! Troy, what've you been telling my baby sister?"

"Nothing. She probably already knows she is a wonderful young lady. She's going places."

"Oh yes, man. She started her business at a young age, a lemonade stand."

They all laughed as they walked toward the car.

CAN'T STOP DESTINY

"Hey, wait for me," Rhonda said, talking to two jocks.

From that time on, Troy and Elisa were impossible to part. They dated up to the end of her sophomore year, at least, until Troy made Elisa break up with him.

✦

"Man, Elisa, where are you taking me? I'm so hungry. My mother was just through cooking. And if you don't stop riding Mrs. Autumn's Lexus the way you are, she is going to skin you alive," Rhonda said, holding on to her seat belt as Elisa was speeding in her mother's car. She always wanted Rhonda around when she was angry. She kept her in control when Stan Junior wasn't around.

"Why are you so angry at Troy? What did he do now?"

"I called him, and some heifer answered his phone. I know where he hangs out on Fridays before he comes to me. So I'm just going to pay him a visit."

As they drove up to his friend's house, the music was booming, and everybody was busy doing their own thing as Elisa walked up, cool and collected, like nothing was wrong. She saw Rodger who was standing in the living room.

"Hi, Rodger, where is Troy? I need to talk to him. It's urgent."

"Hey, Elisa, the last I saw of him, he was over there playing pool. You want me to look around? He should be close by. This house isn't that big."

"That's okay. We'll just look around. Thanks, Rodger."

Elisa was trying not to blow up. She and Troy hadn't been seeing each other that much lately since she'd been working extra days to help her mother, and he was complaining about it more and more. She looked at Rhonda and shook her head as if to say "let's try upstairs."

"Elisa, we can't go up there. This is not our house."

"Are you going or not?"

"Okay, but you're tripping, you know. Troy loves you. Why are you tripping, girl?"

33

As they got closer to another room, she could hear noises that she didn't want to hear. She opened the door, and it was Troy lying in bed with a girl. He opened his mouth and jumped up.

"Hey, baby, it's not the way it looks!" he was screaming, begging her to stop.

"It's just what I knew it was!" Tears started falling.

He hurried and grabbed her before she could run downstairs.

"Please, baby, let me explain!" He pulled her into another room of the house.

"How, how, Troy?" she said, barely able to talk through her tears.

"I love you, Elisa. Listen, listen, please? You don't want to give me any attention. All you worry about is work and studies!"

"This is me, Troy. This was me when you came into my life a year and half ago. I never asked you to change, Troy, even when you promised me you were not doing anything!"

"I'm not. I was just talking to her. This is her parents' home, and she asked me to come up and chill for a little. I told her I had a headache, and we started talking. And then it turned into her telling me how she was attracted to me."

"And that was supposed to be nothing? And why are you letting her answer your phone?"

"I didn't let her answer it. I went to the bathroom, and she told me my phone rang, but it hung up. I knew it couldn't be you because you can't have calls at work. So I didn't check my phone. I just put it aside. She pushed up on me, and I told her we are dating. She started kissing me, and that's when you walked in."

"Troy, Troy, do not play with my intelligence," she pleaded. "I love you, and I can't believe how you betrayed us! It's over, Troy! You and I are not happy anyway! I can't stop who I am for your needs." She cried and tried to walk out.

"Elisa," he whispered as he pulled her close to him. "Baby, you're my air. I can't breathe without you. I promise nothing happened, nothing. Yes, we kissed, but she kissed me. You walked up when I was refusing her. I promise, baby. Yes, I desire more of your time, but I have to learn to adjust, just forgive me!"

CAN'T STOP DESTINY

He held her so tight she couldn't breathe. And all she could think of was that he was in that room and, if she hadn't come in sooner, what really would have happened.

She pulled away softly, eyes swollen and red. She looked up in his eyes. "I'm sorry I can't be what you need me to be. Troy, it's over."

She walked out of the room. The girl looked apologetic, and Rhonda looked like she was about to cry for her friend. As she walked down the stairs, he ran behind her.

"Please, Elisa, give me another chance."

The music stopped. Everyone looked as she walked away, and the car drove off.

⌁⌁⌁

"Troy, thank you for helping me with my things. I hope your friend realizes that you are down here?"

"I texted him. He's on his way down. I see you're still as driven as always."

"Yes, I am, Troy. It's a part of me." She smiled at him.

"And, girl, what! Are you driving a baby Cadillac CTS? This is nice, black with red leather seats? You must be making some pretty good money!"

She laughed.

"Troy, I help keep the insurance up. My father saved money for this since my graduation, and he promised to buy it for me my sophomore year of college. This is my last year. I've had it for two years. And by me having a year of college hours when I got in and also my parents paying for me every summer to take college classes while in high school, it helped me also to get my car this early. After we broke up, I was driven even the more. I didn't want to feel that pain anytime soon."

There was an awkward quietness. They both were thinking about the night they broke up. He felt like he was going to die after she drove off. But the rest of his senior year, they became friends, just without benefits. He even went to her senior prom with her. She came so close to giving in to temptation.

Troy was a sophomore in college, and he still had all the girls going crazy, but her bringing a college guy to the prom made all the girls in her senior class jealous. They even won king and queen of the prom.

"Well, queen, may I have this dance?" Troy asked.

"Yes, you may, my king," she said, bowing before him.

As he held her close, she could not help remembering how close they used to be. As the crowd were screaming, she just held on to him for dear life. He felt her closeness, and it made him blush knowing he was holding one of the most beautiful girls in the prom. When he asked her if he could take her, he was surprised she said yes. But she didn't have a boyfriend. Several boys asked her, but she said no. When Rhonda called him asking him what he was doing and how Elisa didn't want a date, saying she was going stag, he couldn't let that happen and was glad when she agreed that they should go together.

"I can feel your heart beating, young lady," he whispered in her ear.

"It's probably because you are holding me so tight. Not that I mind, but don't get any ideas, young man," she joked.

"I won't," he said, looking down into her eyes. "Elisa, I don't think I will ever get over you. You are something special, lady."

"You are something special too, Troy, but who knows what destiny is for us. Time will tell."

"Yes, it will, baby, yes it will."

As the song stopped, they both looked toward the door. They could hear the girls getting louder as one of the teachers walked in, Mr. Harris. Elisa looked like she had swallowed a ball, and even though she was brown skinned, it looked like her cheeks were dark red from blushing. Troy looked at her as if to say "who is that cat?"

"So who is that you all are crushing over," he said, acting jealous.

CAN'T STOP DESTINY

"That is Mr. Harris. He is a teacher, and he just happens to be one of my favorite teachers. We happened to get close over the last two years. We worked close together with the students and many senior projects, etc. He is just a nice teacher, but these girls have always crushed over him since he's been here. He came the year after you graduated. He is a pretty good teacher. He also helped a lot of students get scholarship help."

"Hey, you make him sound like a king. Don't forget I'm the king tonight!"

As they walked off the floor, the person on the speaker was making an announcement.

"Let's give a hand for the king and queen for tonight. Don't they make a handsome couple?"

As everyone was screaming, Mr. Harris looked at her, and he didn't like the feelings he was feeling for his student and now good friend.

Man, I need to chill, he said, talking to himself. *But she is such an amazing young lady*.

"Hey, are you talking to yourself, man?" one of his colleagues asked, joking.

"No, ma'am. I'm not crazy yet," he joked back.

"Well, Mr. Harris, can I have this dance, sir?" she asked, having a huge crush on him like the students, but he was younger than her. But she didn't care; he was legal.

When they started to dance, the other teachers joined in with them, dancing with the students. The music was slow, and one of Maxwell's songs, "Lovers Only," came on. As he held her close, all the girl students were frowning, and Elisa felt something she did not like feeling about her teacher.

"Hey, he looks like he is really enjoying Ms. Richardson," Troy said, relieved that he wasn't into his students like they wanted him to be.

"Whatever. Let's get a drink and go outside. It's getting a little stuffy in here," she said, boiling inside, knowing Troy was enjoying seeing her jealous and making a fool out of herself.

37

As they were walking out, Mr. Harris saw them going outside. It took everything in him not to make a fool of himself and go after her. He didn't want her to do what most students might do tonight.

Shake it off, man, he said to himself. *She is a student!*

"So what is your plan after this, young lady?" Troy asked, looking handsome and sexy as ever. "If you have nothing to do, I have plans for you."

"Oh, really, and what plan will that be, sir?" She blushed.

"Well, I want to take you somewhere, but you have to trust me and put on a blindfold and don't look until I tell you to."

"Okay, Troy, I'm not into the kinky stuff!"

"Baby, I have never asked you to do nothing you didn't want to do."

"No, you didn't, Troy, and that is probably why we lasted as long as we did, but at the same time, that is why we aren't together also."

"Hey, hey, we are not bringing up the past. I came all the way from New York to be with you, and Columbia is not around the corner."

"Okay. I will trust you this time!" she joked.

As they drove with his top down, he made sure she could not see where he was taking her. As he drove up and parked, she felt like they were falling back.

"Hey, I feel like I'm falling." She grabbed the scarf on her eyes.

"Hey, young lady, no peeping. You promised!"

He walked around and opened the door for her. As she got out of the car, she could smell a familiar smell. He hurried and took it off, knowing she would know if he didn't by the sea smell. As she looked, her mouth fell open. It wasn't like she had never been to the beach, but he took her to a beach house that was on a hill, and you could see the beach from the top of it with the moon shining on it.

"Troy, how, when? I mean…" she said, not able to speak from the view.

"I called my uncle when you agreed to let me escort you, and he let me borrow their beach home. They live in California, but they bought this for when they come here and visit my grandparents. I thought you would like this being you are a private person and all."

She was speechless.

CAN'T STOP DESTINY

"Troy, this is amazing, and you know it. You are so wrong for this. But I love it!"

He picked her up as they walked in. He had the music programmed when he clapped to play Maxwell's song "Now."

He took her and sat her on the sofa. She was overwhelmed, and he could see it in her eyes. She had that look she always had when he did something she least expected from him. He brought her over a smoothie he had made for her earlier. It was not frozen because of the special cup he put it in; it was just right.

He gave her the drink and asked her, "What should we toast to?"

"Graduation, of course." She smiled. "Troy, this is the stuff that made me love you. You know that, don't you?"

"Yep." He laughed and then looked at her blushing, then "Till the Cops Come Knocking" came on by Maxwell.

"Okay, what's up with Maxwell? You know any girl with sense loves his music. It's like liquor without the cup!"

"Nothing, baby. I just wanted to make our night—your night—remarkable and a night you can tell our grandchildren about."

"Our grandchildren, there you go fantasizing again."

Troy did not smile. He did not talk. He took her glass and pulled her closer.

"Elisa, you are everything a man could want, baby. And if I can only have you for this blessed night, all this is worth it. I will always love you and want you, girl. But I wish I was a part of your future. And if I am good, and if I'm not, tonight will be in your memory forever and a part of me in it also."

He reached over, put her drink down, and kissed her softly. She could not help but respond to his advances. This was Troy, of all people. No woman could resist him, not even Elisa.

She pulled in closer as he whispered in her ear, "Elisa, I want you, and you know this. May I please be your first? If I'm not, can I make you feel like I'm your first?"

"Yes, Troy, yes. I want you to be my first."

He took her in his arms and carried her downstairs into the bedroom that had roses on the bed and wine glasses on the table with grape wine next to it.

"I'll let you get comfortable," he said as he went in the restroom to get his condoms.

As she was lying there nervous, she started talking to herself. *I can't believe Troy is going to be my first! And he is really putting the icing on thick.* She looked out the window that had no curtains, and she could see the beach water waving by it. *I would be crazy not to make love to him, and he is my first true love.*

As she was about to get undressed, her cell phone went off. She checked the message.

> I want to congratulate you on being the most beautiful queen I've seen in a long time. I hope you will be safe tonight and enjoy the memories that will last a lifetime.

She jumped. It was Mr. Harris. Every emotion she felt left that very second. Troy walked out, looking amazing. He had a towel wrapped around his bottom area. And she could see from the way it looked he was ready.

"Troy, I can't!"

"What!" He almost stopped breathing! "What happened to change your mind in ten minutes?

"I'm just not ready!"

"Are you all right?

"I want this to be a memory I can tell my grandchildren about with my husband."

"Okay, Elisa." He walked toward her, and she could still feel his welcoming hello.

"So let's just go in the kitchen and get something to eat. I have plenty, and in fact, I have your favorite. My mother cooked it—spaghetti."

"No, she did not!"

"Yes, she did," he said, smiling but very disappointed.

"Troy, I'm sorry. Maybe in the future, if fate allows. But this will be a memory for my grandchildren. I think you better go put some clothes on before you get a cold," she joked.

CHAPTER 3

"Why are you quiet, Troy? You never were quiet growing up. Mice got your tongue?" she said, trying stop the tension they both felt. As he was putting her things in her car, all he could think was the night he almost made her the woman he knew she would be.

"I'm not quiet for nothing. I was just admiring the fact that you're still as beautiful as the night I almost made magic with you."

"Magic, you say. So you think you would've made magic that night, Mr. Troy?" She laughed out loud.

"Yes, I know I would have everything. That night was magical, girl, and you know it. I just needed the icing on the cake, that I would have you in my arms, in my bed."

She felt awkward, but she still was waiting for Mr. Right.

"Troy, that was a magical night. I still think of it when I'm thinking of how that day will be. I'm hoping it will be as wonderful as you made it that night. Your wife is going to be blessed."

"You still a virgin, girl! That does not happen no more, not in these days and times. Where do you get that supernatural strength from, girl! Please share, please?"

"You're crazy, Troy, and it is not easy, believe me. I think that is why God put this drive in me. It keeps me faithful to him. Know this. I am not dead. I do have feelings for the other sex."

"Thank God. I thought you were trying to be a…well, I won't say it. You're too beautiful for me to insult you."

"Troy! You better not be asking what I think you're asking me. No, no, I am strictly a woman needing a man, in every way"!

"Yes! So there is hope for me then."

"I know you're not still holding your breath, Mr. Troy."

"Yes, girl!"

They both started laughing. Elisa started talking, trying to change the subject before she did something she would regret because Troy was still sexy at the age of twenty-three.

"So when was the last time you've been to sweet Pensacola, Florida? I miss home. When I first left, I used to go home at least three times a month. But once I started work study program offered at the London Study Center in the social sciences PSI CHI organization on human and animal research, I didn't have time to go home. And that extra money helped me not to beg as much."

She laughed, still trying to keep the pressure low. This was Troy, of all people, her first love.

"I told you driven, driven. I think I will learn a thing or two from you, ma'am. I'm still partying. I work hard. I'm actually the honcho in the business I'm working with. I still play baseball, but you know, my major was computer science. It keeps me busy, Elisa," he said, staring at her as if he was trying to look through her soul.

"Um, yes." She surely was trying not to notice his staring at her. It always made her want to give in to his advances. "Well, I'm glad to hear you are using that free money."

"Yes, I am, and I see you are too."

"Yes, I am. A long time coming, but it was worth it. I'm almost out of here. I found a building for my business. I will be moving back close to my family. I want to help my mother's hospital with some of their load also."

"So what business is this again, young lady"?

"I will have a practice for patients with mental problems, a family practice. I also will be helping youth with mental problems with the system. I also will have a team of students that will be graduating

CAN'T STOP DESTINY

working with me. Over the four years, I saved enough capital to actually own my business after the first two years."

"Man, girl, your driven ways have gotten you what you were destined for. I'm so proud of you, even though your focus tore us apart. Elisa, I'm so happy for you, and the way I'm feeling, I hope I won't be your first patient," he joked.

"Troy, will you stop flirting? You know we just weren't meant."

She looked away and hit the key to open the trunk. He helped her put the rest of her things in, seeing that she was trying to leave and not get caught up in the past, at least with him.

"Thanks, Troy," she said as he opened her door.

He grabbed her in his arms, wanting to at least feel what he couldn't have. At least not now, he was hoping.

"Elisa, if it won't be me, some man is going to be so blessed, woman."

"Troy, some woman is going to be blessed also. I will always love you. I will see you in the Pensu soon," she joked.

As she drove, she was looking at him in her rearview mirror. *He still hasn't grown up, but boy, he sure got the looks. Someone is really going to be blessed!* She busted out laughing as she speeded off in her baby Cadillac.

The phone rang, and she wanted it to stop. She had a long night studying for finals. It continued to ring. So Elisa grabbed it. It hit the floor. She jumped up and grabbed the phone.

"Hello," she whispered, not knowing if she was answering it or dreaming.

"Hi, sis. This is your big brother. I'm in Tallahassee. I'm coming to get you and take you downtown. I need to talk to you about something important."

"Okay, but let me come to, from dream world. I'm not dreaming, am I, bro?"

"No, sis. Wake up. This is important. I'll be there in a few."

She pulled the cover over her head and fell back to sleep. She had just gone to sleep at 2:00 a.m., studying for her finals. As she was lying down, she heard a knock at the door. She jumped up, remembered that her brother had called.

"Oh no, who is it?"

"Stan. Sis, can you open the door? It's hot out here."

"Hi, bro," she said, barely able to talk. She gave him a big hug. "Come in. I'm sorry, big bro. I was studying until this morning. This better be important. I love you, but you will be in trouble, buster." She smiled, glad to see her big brother.

"Come on, I wouldn't drive here if it wasn't important. You know I fly, but after this weekend, Uncle Sam is going to be keeping me busy. So I wanted to drive and think. The money is worth it, but that is not what I need right now. I need to talk to you about it."

"Okay, okay. Let me get my one cup of coffee please. Come, have a seat."

Her coffee pot had a timer on it that she sat before she went to sleep, knowing she would need it if she was going to go take a test at 1:00 p.m. As she was looking at him while fixing her coffee to drink, Stan looked at her with a much-concerned look.

"Well, it's like this, sis. I did something that I hope I didn't do. I slept with this lady, not knowing her husband was in the service with me."

"Uh-oh, and?"

"And she thinks she is pregnant."

"Oh no, Stan. What you did, you forgot about the law!"

"Well, the man she is married to is one of my sergeants, and man, she wants to kill my baby."

"What! Stan, this is a nightmare. So…what…I mean how…I mean, Stan…oh my god, how'd you let this happen? Do Mom and Dad know? Don't answer that dumb question. You wouldn't have driven all this way."

"Man, sis, I don't know what to do, but I need to talk to someone before I go crazy. She won't listen to me. She is afraid to tell her husband, even though they are separated. We met at an after party. She is so beautiful any man would have jumped to her. I can't believe I didn't use my protection! Man, I don't want to lose my job. Even though he can't hurt me because of my rank, he can try to make my life a living hell."

"Okay, Stan, she is a grown-up. You can't stop her. It's her body! Well, I don't mean to sound cruel, but you are going have to pray and

CAN'T STOP DESTINY

wait for the will of God. It's your baby, true, but unless you're ready to get a lawyer and fight her not to kill the baby, there is nothing you can do. I'm so sorry, Stan."

She walked over to hold her brother, her best friend, and realized that she has a nephew or niece on the way. Her heart became heavy, and she was thinking of a plan.

Hey, she said to herself, *this is what I major, the mind. I can try to talk to her if she'll let me.*

As he was holding her tight, he was about to cry. He pulled away.

"Hey, sis, that's why I need my best friend." He smiled.

"I love you too. Now listen. I have a plan, if you're okay with it."

"Anything, sis, anything right now. I'm desperate!"

"Where is this lady?"

"At this moment, she is in Miami with her family. She's been there since she has been separated, and since she found out about the baby, she won't go back to her home."

"So they still live together?"

"No, um, she still has the house. He moved in a crib by himself, until they decide to get a divorce or not."

"After my finals, which is today, big brother, let's fly to Miami, and I'll make the reservations. You forgot I'm a psychologist." She laughed.

"Yeah, man, I forgot, and it won't cost me nothing!"

"Oh, it's going cost you because you are paying for the plane ticket and I pay for the hotel and we go half on the rental."

"Hey, you sound like you've been planning this before I came!"

"No, big bro. I'm a doctor, and I always plan to win. I care about the minds of people, and it's something God put in me. So with that being said, let's meet tonight, and I will have everything planned and ready to go."

"So I'll bring my things up and shower and get my thoughts together. That's why you, my big little sister, you always know what I need."

He kissed her on the forehead and went out smiling like one of the twins. Elisa jumped into the shower. As she was getting out, she heard the phone ring. She tried to go reach it, but Stan answered.

"Hi, Elisa Martin residence, how can I help you?"

"Hello, this is Rhonda, her friend. May I speak to her please?"

"Rhonda girl, you don't recognize your brother's voice?"

"Stan Junior! What are you doing in Tallahassee, Florida?"

"I'm here on an emergency. I need my little sister's advice."

"Oh, so you need a shrink." She busted out laughing. "You do know she is a head doctor now."

"Yea, yea, I know. I guess I need a shrink than woman problem."

"What woman problem is going to make you drive down there? Aren't you on leave visiting your parents?"

"Yes, but the twins are keeping them busy. I needed my best friend, and it just happened my best friend is in Tallahassee, my sister, a shrink." He laughed. "So do you want to talk to her or keep flirting with me?"

"Flirting! I know you wish, big bro. Yes, let me talk to her."

"Elisa, I'm going to clean up. It's your friend Rhonda."

"Hey, sis. what's up, and what's the call for? You're all right, I hope. We haven't talked in a while."

"Well, it's like this. I'm bored, and all work and no play is making Rhonda a bored soul. Well, what are you doing?"

"I'm almost through with finals, and Stan Junior and I are flying to Miami in the morning to take care of some business. Hey, we can all make it a fun weekend. I need the downtime until graduation comes up. And I'll be starting my business soon I won't have no time for play."

"Like you have time now. That's why I don't hear or bother you. You are so busy and driven, Elisa. If I wasn't your best friend, I'll mess over you just like Troy did."

"Ooh, that was a cold blow, Rhonda. What made you go there?"

"Because I saw that hunk yesterday while I was shopping, him and a bunch of his fine friends, and he told me he just saw you and how you are still driven, and even though it turns him on, it pushes him away too."

"Troy wasn't pushing away, my friend. He was trying to push on. I pushed him off."

CAN'T STOP DESTINY

"Again, poor Troy. You figure, a woman leaves you in front of all your friends, you won't want to be bothered anymore. And he didn't even get the gold after all that money he spent on you for your prom. Poor Troy Andrews."

"Poor Troy—girl, I'm saving myself for the platinum, not fake silver! Troy almost got it, but you already know why he didn't. I tell you everything."

"Yep, so when was the last time you heard from your baby daddy, Mr. William Harris?

"I haven't. The last I heard, my father said he is still teaching, but he didn't see him much after that. My mother said she heard he was leaving the States to teach at a college. One of her friends whose grandchild was in his class told her."

"Man, I know you wanted to jump on that, but timing is everything I guess."

Elisa got quiet. She always did when someone talked about Mr. William Harris. She always felt the same feelings she felt the last time they talked. But she figured, since he hadn't tried to find her, he realized she was just not the one. So it gave her even more drive to go after her dreams.

"Elisa, are you still there?"

"Oh yes, girl. I was just thinking about William and wondering how he is doing."

"Won't you call him?"

"No, if it's meant, fate will make it happen. But to change the subject, do you want to fly with us to Miami or not?"

"Elisa, you know, I guess I can go. I have nothing else to do. Will we hit the beaches while we're there? I'm tired of George Beach. I need a change of scenery."

"Okay, we'll be there in the morning. We are leaving early. We will arrive at Miami International Airport around 11:00 a.m. We are renting a Bentley. You know my brother. If I try to give him a common car, he has a fit. A rose like his father."

They both laughed as they hung up the phone.

CHAPTER 4

As the TV came on loudly, William jumped up, forgetting to turn the sound on the TV down from the alarm he set to wake him. He was in Paris, France. He couldn't believe he was offered such an honor. He guessed learning other languages paid off. As he got up to drink a warm cup of coffee, he glanced over to the TV he had on for an alarm. The weather man was talking.

"Weather today in Paris will be beautiful, yet there is a storm rising in the Gulf, but it won't interfere with the comfortable spring weather. Might need an umbrella since this is the rainy month."

"Yes, this is a weekend to enjoy the beach before it gets scorching hot," another announcer mentioned. "Time for all those graduates and a shout-out to them all—Florida, Texas, California—college and high school graduates where the weather is almost always perfect. And don't forget the high school and college graduates in Paris."

As the announcers were talking, William couldn't hear about Paris because he started thinking of Elisa. He was wondering, did she remember their agreement? William blushed, realizing now he was not ashamed to think of her anymore. He knew she was now a twenty-year-old woman, about to be twenty-one.

She's probably not thinking about a twenty-five-year-old man, almost twenty-six, he was thinking to himself.

"Well, she should be graduating soon," he said, talking out loud. "Look at me, I'm acting like a high school kid, but I was really intrigued with that woman, I must admit. If fate allows, I will try harder the next time. Well, let me get ready for work."

As William walked down the hallway to his classroom, all the ladies were whispering and blushing, and they were talking in French. Since he was an American and young looking for a professor, they thought he was a student that couldn't speak French.

"If I had that on my plate, I would eat it all up," one of the students said as she walked in class behind him.

He blushed, and as she sat down, all the women around her were laughing with her. As he entered the room to write his name on the board, they all looked as if they swallowed an egg.

"Hello," he said as he wrote his name on the board in French and English. "I'm your professor, and I will enjoy teaching you history, for you are paying your hard-earned money to learn more about many great countries."

"Oh my god," one of the students said, speaking in French but not planning for him to hear.

"Hello, and how can I assist God with you today?" he blushed, making all the women blush in their seats.

"No, sir." She spoke in French.

"I have three languages, thanks to my persistent parents— English, Spanish, and French—which I made close to straight As in. So if you want to talk in English or French, please indulge me? I'm here to help you, not to intimidate, but I will be speaking in French since I'm in Paris." He smiled. "Can you please turn in your books to chapter one," he said, blushing at how the students always took him for one of them. It made him think of Elisa again.

As classes were over for the day, one of his coworkers asked him to go out for happy hour. He hesitated at first because he wasn't ready to get friendly in a strange country, and he wanted to feel the place first.

As he was through for the day, one of his coworkers asked him out to eat. They often talked during teachers' breaks and held conversations since they both were from the States.

"All right, man, I'm down. I need to familiarize myself anyway."

"Man, where I'm about to take you, they love American men. And you will have so much fun you forget American women."

"Really, man? I need that place then."

He thought to himself, *I really need to get over Elisa. This is probably what I need.* He was trying to convince himself. As they entered, the ambiance of the place had a welcoming feeling. As they sat down, he noticed the beautiful women as far as you could see.

"Man," he said as he sat down, "these women are beautiful. Too many for one man."

"Yes, sir, my friend. And man, they are ready to oblige you, if you know what I mean."

"Yes, I do, but I need to go home. Man, who knows what these women have."

"Okay, I know you aren't a virgin from America," he joked.

"No, I'm not, man. But hey, looks aren't everything."

"Man, I came over here for the same reason you did, to make more real money. But if I get me some hello while I'm saying goodbye, if you know what I mean, I'm okay with that too."

William smiled, not answering. It was amazing to him how many people were speaking English, but he could still hear French, and if he listened closely, he could hear a little Spanish. As he was talking in his mind, the waiter walked over, smiling. He spoke in French.

"Sirs, the ladies over there sent you this bottle of wine."

William blushed.

"Sir, tell them thank you," his coworker answered in English.

"Oh, so you are American?" He spoke in English.

"Yes, sir, we are."

"So are you students at the university?"

They both smiled, trying not to seem childish, wanting to laugh.

"Sir, we both teach at the university."

"Man!" he said, amazed at them. "Well, sir, I thought you were a student." He was looking at William.

"Well, long story, sir, but I'm old enough to teach. But can you tell the ladies we appreciate their hospitality?"

As he was about to go tell them, they walked over.

"Hello," they said in French.

"Hello," his coworker Sam said in French, wanting to sound sexy and charming.

CAN'T STOP DESTINY

"Hello," William said in English, letting them know he was not from Paris.

"So can we join you, sirs? Not wanting to impose on your downtime, but you are good to the eyes," one said, looking William up and down.

"Please do join us!" Sam said, smiling hard.

"So who is your handsome friend?" the other lady asked.

"My name is William, and I can talk French," he joked as he said it in French.

"Hey, so what are you ladies doing on a nice evening like this?" Sam asked.

"Looking for some men like you to keep us company. Would you like to dance?"

They were playing an American artist, and the sound was really on point.

"Hey, come on, love," Sam said as he grabbed her and went on the floor.

William looked at the other woman and smiled.

"So are you going to ask me to dance or just keep making me blush with that sexy dimple?"

"Would you like this dance?" William asked softly and sexily, trying not to sound desperate.

"Man, if you keep talking like that, you are going to have to suck me up with a straw."

"I don't want to do that," he joked.

As they entered the floor, the song changed to a slow song. William pulled her close to him. As she pulled into him, she felt so at home. As the music was almost over, he rubbed her long hair gently because it was down her back where his hands weren't planning to be.

She whispered in his ear, "So what is your name again?"

"William."

"And what is your name?"

"Lisa."

He stopped dancing, and she looked up at him.

"Are you all right?" she asked, looking confused.

"Um, yes." He grabbed her hand as they walked to the table. He couldn't believe he met a woman named Lisa.

As Sam and the other lady came and sat down, they noticed the awkwardness.

"Hey, what did we miss?" Sam asked, staring at William as if to say "man, don't mess this up for me."

"Nothing," William answered quickly. "I just noticed the music was stopping."

"Oh, that's what it was?" the lady asked. "I thought you had seen a ghost."

"No. Would you like another glass of this wonderful wine you blessed us with?" William said, trying to change the subject.

As the night was almost over, he looked at his watch and noticed the time was well spent.

"Well, ladies, I have to go to work in the morning. Can I walk you to your cars?" William asked, trying not to sound obvious.

"Well," Sam said, knowing he was about to get lucky. "Well, I'll be walking this one out, and I'll see you at work tomorrow, buddy, if you know what I mean."

"Yes, I do," William said, smiling. "Well, I'll do that my friend. The offer still stands, ma'am, if you need me to walk you out."

"Yes, I will appreciate it," she said, wishing he would go home with her.

As they reached her car, she pulled him close to her. "You don't have to go home, unless you really want to?"

"Yes, I really need to be prepared. I'm a teacher, and it's not the same as teaching high school students."

"So, William, you are a professor at the university?" she asked.

"Yes, I am. It's my first day, and I really enjoyed the challenge of it so far."

"So can I give you my number? And when you're ready for a nightcap or something, you can give me a call," she ended by speaking in English.

"Okay, I appreciate it, and I will call if I need one. Thank you."

She pulled him close to her, and she tried to kiss him. And he kissed her on the forehead.

CAN'T STOP DESTINY

"Good night," she said, feeling insulted because she was beautiful, and most men begged to go home with her.

As William entered his apartment, he thought about how beautiful that woman was, and he couldn't believe he sent her home alone.

What is wrong with me? I haven't talked to Elisa in years, three exactly, he said to himself as he took his clothes off to take a shower. *The last time I made love to a beautiful woman, I almost called her Elisa. I need to get over her. What is the connection to that lady?*

CHAPTER 5

As they entered Miami International Airport, and the plane was stopping, Rhonda made a joke about her ears popping. "I asked you to chew the gum," Elisa said. "But no. Because it was sugarless gum, you didn't want it."

"I'm not on a diet. I still have my high school figure. Give me some sugar, please!"

They all busted out laughing.

"Girl, you have jokes, but I need you to behave down here," Stan Junior pleaded.

"Why are you asking me to behave? You're the one having jokes and other men's wives."

"Hey, I told you that as a little sister. You're going throw that in my face?"

"No, no, just when you don't let me be me."

"Meaning silly, right?"

"Can you guys stop tripping?" Elisa said, looking through her planner. "I'm trying to figure out which way to go get the rental. We can catch a shuttle, I was told. I'm renting a 2005 Mercedes Benz CLK Class Convertible. I was going to rent a newer Bentley, but you know what, I keep that money for the hotel. Stan Junior, you and your father can pay $1,400 or more for a Bentley, but not me." She was joking but meant every word.

CAN'T STOP DESTINY

When they reached the rental place, the salesman handed the keys to her.

"Oh no, you can give those keys to the Benz to my uppity brother who will be doing the driving. He loves living large."

"And it's okay with me, sis. I'm not uppity, little Elisa. My parents raised me to want the best. So I get the best."

"Oh, please don't make me go there!" Rhonda said, laughing, thinking about why they were there.

Stan looked at her and his sister. As he was about to answer Rhonda back, his phone went off. It was her. Elisa looked in his eyes, and she knew he was getting that fear back. She hated to see that in her brother's eyes, which was why she was making a last-minute trip a week before her college graduation. She loved Stan Junior that much.

"Stan," she asked as he was answering the phone. "You are going be okay?"

He just shook his head, saying yes with a half smile as he walked off a little to answer the phone.

"Hi," he said in his handsome and masculine voice.

"Hi, Stan. I guess you made it. Is your sister with you?"

"Yes, she is. We brought our play sister along also. She needed to get away. Not to change the subject, but where can we meet you?"

"Well, I'm still on the beachfront. I guess I can meet you at your hotel."

"We'll be staying in the Delano Hotel. It's on the beach also. Call me when you get there to see if we made it there yet."

"So you think your sister can change my mind, Stan? You must have that much faith in her abilities you spent time and money to come all this way. I know you. You only want the best. You're probably riding in a new Bentley?"

"No, my sister rented the car, and we're driving a Mercedes convertible."

"What! Oh yes, I need to talk to her if she convinced you of that. For the baby's sake, that's the only reason I agreed to talk to her. Stan, this is better for everyone."

"Who is everyone, Carolyn? You and your husband? What about our child, Carolyn? Wait, wait," Stan Junior said, getting more

55

upset. "I didn't come all this way to argue. I promise to let you handle what's best for you, but don't expect me to love it, but I really thank you for letting Elisa have this chance to talk to you."

Carolyn paused before talking because even though she could hear the hurt in his voice, she really was doing it for all their good, and she still could feel the love that she has for him. He had broken up with her when he found out that she was married to his boss, even though they were separated. He could not handle the secret she kept for so long, feeling that he couldn't trust her, leaving her vulnerable and still in love with him.

"Stan, I will see you and your sister in a few, and I will try, baby, just for you. I promise."

He looked at Elisa and Rhonda, and they could see that he was still in love with her. They felt vulnerable and sad for him, giving each other that look as if to say he's in trouble.

As they drove with the top down, the wind blowing through their hair, the girls were enjoying seeing how beautiful Miami was. Elisa remembered how her parents would bring them down there twice a year for their father's business meetings. While he was in meetings, they would shop and spend time on the beach. Meanwhile, Stan Junior was thinking about Carolyn and their last day together.

⁓∞⧜∞⁓

"Will you stop teasing me, sweetheart? Come on, let me see what you got on," he kept asking, lying down on the floor rug, waiting for her to come out.

"Hi," she said as she peeked out the door. "What's up, my big huggy bear?"

She walked out in an all-black see-through baby doll gown.

"Man, baby, you look good enough to eat," he said as he pulled her down on top of him. Carolyn blushed as he gently asked her a question. "Baby, it's so beautiful. Can I please try it on later?" he joked as he gently took it off and laid her down softly. He made sweet love to her, and all she could do was cry as he did what he did so many times so well. He was the best lover she had ever had, and

CAN'T STOP DESTINY

she couldn't lose him. As they were finishing up, he looked at her in his arms.

"Carolyn, I love you so much, sweetheart. One day, you will be my wife if the fate allows. And I will make you an honest woman. I can't keep giving you all of big poppa, and you're not my wife."

"Big poppa. Okay, baby, you can be big poppa. And by the way, I love you too, and one day when you're ready, we will be man and wife."

She paused in her mind as she said it, knowing too well that she was already married. The guilt was tearing her apart. She knew she had to tell him, but how? As he got up, he pulled her up off the floor and walked her to the shower. As the water was slowly running down her back, he rubbed her softly and asked why she was so quiet.

"Stan, I have to talk to you, and it's something I should have told you for a while now. But the more time we spent together, the more I knew I was falling in love with you, and I just can't lose you, Stan."

"Hey! You are scaring me, baby," he said, drying her off.

She looked at his beautiful body and his sexy eyes and his soft gestures, and she was afraid to tell him anything.

"What are you trying to tell me?" he said as he walked off, getting them a drink. He turned the music on, some of Luther Vandross's best hits, which didn't make what she was trying to tell him any easier. As "Always and Forever" came on, she started to cry, and she held him so tight he couldn't pull her off to look into her eyes.

"Carolyn, now you're really scaring me!"

He put the drinks aside and sat her on the sofa next to him.

"Stan, I'm so, so, sorry," she said, barely catching her words to talk to him. "Stan, I'm married!"

Stan stood up and walked toward the patio. He looked outside as the ocean waves were dashing downstairs. From the apartment patio, he could see her standing. He felt as if he was looking at a stranger.

"Carolyn, tell me this is a joke, girl! This is not happening, not to us, not to me!" he screamed, not turning around but talking to her reflection.

"Stan, I was going to tell you after our second date, but when I found out that my husband is your sergeant, I was already falling in love with you! I knew you would leave me, so I tried my best to wait until the time was right."

"Right! The time would never be right, girl. You are married. You should have never allowed this to get this far! Carolyn, girl, I can't believe this!" he said, hitting on the patio. As he turned around, she could see the tears in his eyes.

"Stan," she said as she ran up to him. "Please forgive me, baby, please!"

He took a deep breath as he was trying to compose himself. All she could notice were his biceps because he still was standing with just a towel wrapped around him. He was fit. Being in the air force, he stayed in the gym. And looking at him, he looked like he was about to burst trying to keep his cool.

"So you know it's over, right, Carolyn?"

"Why, Stan? We are getting a divorce soon. I promise, baby. Please don't throw what we have away!"

"Away! You did that all by yourself."

He walked past her, looking for his pants.

"Stan Martin, I'm pregnant!"

Stan stopped. He looked at her, and he felt like he was holding his breath.

"I know God is punishing me for this affair. This is not happening. You are not pregnant. How could you put all this on me at one time, girl!"

"That's what was taking me so long to come out of the bathroom. I was taking a pregnancy test again. I had to make sure. Stan, I am two months late, baby," she said as the tears were falling.

"Carolyn, Carolyn," he whispered. "You are having my child? How do you know it's mine?"

"I know. I haven't been with him in months."

"Oh my god, Carolyn. This is the best thing out of this."

"No, it isn't, Stan! I am having an abortion."

"What!" He ran up to her, grabbing her, kissing her in the mouth. "Baby, baby," he said, crying. "Don't kill our child, Carolyn, please, please!

CAN'T STOP DESTINY

She held him. "Stan, he's your boss. He is ignorant, that's why we separated!"

Stan stood and stopped crying. "Who is he?"

"Sergeant Mitchell!"

He got quiet as he looked at her. "Mitchell, man, Mitchell! He's not just my sergeant. He's my boss, Carolyn. Dang, baby, why!"

"I didn't know, Stan! I didn't know when I met you at the after party. Mitchell and I had been separated for six months. Our marriage was over even before that!"

"Carolyn, don't kill my child, please! You can't compare that with him and us. It was over. He will understand. It was a coincidence. Carolyn, please don't kill my baby?"

She ran up to him. They both cried, and she said, "It's best, Stan."

"Carolyn, it's over. I can't be with you. You kept this from me, and to top that off, you made love to me. And now you're having my baby, and you want to kill it too. I'm gone. It's over. I'll be back when you come to your senses. That's a life in you though, so think about that please. Don't do it, just think about it. Give it a moment before you do it."

"I will. I promise. And can you forgive me and think about us, Stan? I know you love me. Let's take it one day at a time."

"Carolyn, it's over. That I do know."

<hr>

"Hey, where'd you go, big brother? You do know where the hotel is?" Elisa asked, noticing he had left them for a moment. He had not talked since they drove off from the airport.

"I'm okay, sis. I was just thinking about Carolyn and how we got to this point. Sis, we connected in ways I thought I would never connect with a woman. To keep that from me, and then she seemed so selfish trying to kill my child, as if this is a game to her, I'm surprised she agreed to even talk to you. Maybe that's some kind of game also."

"All I know is, if you want, I will handle her for you, big bro!" Rhonda said, coming to his defense.

"I don't think she is like that at all," Elisa said, making him almost run the red light.

"How could you believe that, Elisa!" he said, angry and confused at the same time.

"Well, bro, the reason I say this is, for one, she agreed to see me. And my brother would not fall in love with a woman unless she was a remarkable woman. Sounds like a woman that fell in love with a remarkable man and did not plan for her feelings to go as far and as soon as they did. I mean, I'm just saying I'm only a four-year psychology major." She smiled at him. Noticing it made him think and blush a little. "Hey, Rhonda, don't you agree?" Elisa said, hoping for her encouragement in it all.

"Well, Stan Junior, she does have a point. I think you are being a little stubborn, like, you know…hey, maybe the girl is probably afraid. I mean, I'm just saying."

"Oh no, I know you two were ready to handle her five minutes ago, not ganging up on me?"

He kept driving, and he started thinking. And he forgot what made her so special and the woman he was thinking about bringing home to his parents. He never brought women around his family. If they met one of his lady friends, it was always by accident—in the restaurant, in the store, but never on purpose. He always told his mother, "I don't want women walking in and out of your life."

As he drove up to the hotel, he saw her car parked in front. As he got valet parking, he asked the bellboy to bring their luggage up to their room.

"Sis, I had a small meeting room reserved, and Carolyn should be there waiting for you."

"How'd you know she's there?" she said, looking confused.

"I talked to her and asked her to meet us here, and I told the concierge, when she arrives, to escort her to one of the meeting rooms."

"So you handled everything, big bro. Can I at least freshen up, please? I'm meeting her for the first time, and I don't want to look tired."

CAN'T STOP DESTINY

"Tired, tired isn't the word. I can't catch a man looking like this," Rhonda said, joking.

"Okay, go up, ladies. Here are your keys. I'll be up in a moment."

As they entered the room, they couldn't believe the view from the window. Elisa made sure to get a room by the beachfront.

"Man, Elisa, this is awesome! Only you could find a room like this. I don't even want to know what you are paying for it."

"Well, it's connecting rooms to Stan's room. So for three days, it's only $550 with tax per day."

"Girl, your mother sure taught you both how to have the best."

"My mother—it's my father, girl. We couldn't go out of town unless he rented Bentleys. Do you know how much? They run $1,300, if not more, a day! Stan does the same thing. I think they save for it because my mother will get an SUV in a minute, Cadillac Escalade, or a Lincoln Town Car. It had to look good too, but she spent her money on shopping."

"Man, I'm going to enjoy this hotel. I'm going to use Stan's shower."

As the women were upstairs refreshing, Stan was sitting at the bar, nervous about seeing Carolyn again.

"Man, you saw that beauty who just went into that meeting room?" one of the bartenders said. "I'd like to make her my wifey." He joked, "I'd be stroking that all night long."

"Excuse me, sir, but she already has a husband."

"Oh, man, I'm sorry. I didn't know. Your wife is very beautiful. You are a lucky man."

"She is not my wife. She is another man's wife," Stan said sarcastically.

The bartender looked away, feeling awkward.

"Well, man, if you want a refill, let me know."

"No, thank you, man," Stan said, feeling jealous and grateful at the same time.

As he walked out of the bar, he noticed the door to the meeting room was open. He walked over and looked in. He saw her standing by the window, looking out at the kids swimming at the pool, drinking her favorite drink. She was in a sundress that formed every shape a man could imagine. As she turned toward the door, she looked at him, and he walked in and sat at the table near the door.

"Hi, Carolyn, I hope your arrival was smooth. I asked them to make sure you were comfortable until we arrived. And how is my baby?"

She walked over to him as he stood there, and she fell into his arms, crying.

"Stan, I love you and this baby. Why are you treating me like the enemy?" She couldn't control her tears. He sat her down and went to close the door.

"I'm sorry, baby. I realize that the woman I fell in love with could not make this kind of decision unless she was trying to protect us." He pulled her up closer to him. "Carolyn, I'm sorry for how I acted the last time we talked. Please tell me you forgive me?"

"Stan, you mean this? You understand?"

"Understand that you are doing what you feel is right for us all, but Carolyn, that baby is a human, and it's a part of us!"

"I don't want my child having anything to do with my husband. We aren't divorced yet, and Mitchell will try to control me and this baby just to get to you. And legally, he can because we are still married. That is why I'm still going through with it."

Stan got up and walked out the room. His heart could not handle hearing it or seeing her, knowing she was going to kill their child. As he walked out, eyes bloodshot, Elisa and Rhonda were coming off the elevator. They were dressed up from head to toe. The bartenders were trying their best to convince them to sit and talk over drinks. Elisa hurried up and said "no, thanks," seeing her brother and trying to get to him.

"Stan, what happened? You look like you're about to explode."

"She's in there, sis. Please talk some sense in her for your family's sake, please!"

She looked at his red eyes, knowing he was about to cry.

"Stan, I will try my best. Please go upstairs and rest. I'll be up when we're done. Rhonda, I guess you will stay here and keep those gentlemen company."

"Yes, I will I keep your seat warm, my friend. Go take care of my big brother's problem."

CAN'T STOP DESTINY

As Elisa walked in, she closed the door behind her. She could see that Carolyn had been crying. She sat at the head of the conference table. And her heart went out to them both.

"Hi, Carolyn, is it? Please have a seat. The floor will not rise if you sit for a moment," she joked.

Carolyn sat down and smiled lightly, needing to feel a sense of living, because at that moment, she was feeling very tired and sad. She hadn't slept well since she told Stan Junior, and he left her in her fears.

"Hi, you must be Elisa. I heard a lot about you. Stan loves you so much. He said you are his best friend and big little sister."

They both laughed.

"Yes, he's been saying that since middle school. All we had were each other until the twins came. My parents took us to the engineering company where they worked often, so we weren't around other kids but at school. So we became real close. But enough about us. It's you that needs me now, and I'm ready to be there for you if you allow."

"Well, I really don't know where to start. It's pretty self-explanatory. I'm pregnant by your brother, and he wants me to keep the baby. But I think for all concerned in this situation, it would be better to have an abortion."

She burst into tears again. Elisa got up and went to get her some tissue. She sat down and grabbed her hand, being very sympathetic.

"Why would you think killing your baby would make it better for everyone?"

"Well, what I didn't tell Stan is, my husband, Mitchell, knows already about the affair, and he told me if I don't call it off, he is going to make it hard for Stan. He also decided, even though we are in the process of getting a divorce, that if I keep the baby, he is going to prolong the divorce by making up a lot of lies to keep me away from Stan. So if I keep the baby, I will be in a marriage that has been over for some time now. Mitchell was very mentally abusive. I just want to get him out of my life, and I won't bring a baby into it. I just can't!"

"Carolyn, it sounds to me that he is winning. Not only is he abusive to you, but now he is controlling your body and your seed, my brother's seed. He cannot keep having that kind of power. I believe Stan can handle whatever situation Mitchell brings his way. But you will have to stand up, if not for yourself, then for that innocent baby, a baby that won't have a prayer if you don't realize that God has freed you from this man, but you keep giving him the power. Usually, when men are mentally abusive, there is a coward behind him, and he is only talk. But you have been feeding that seed, and you're keeping it alive. Tell me how you even left in the first place?"

"One day, I just got tired of his yelling at me, treating me for years like I am one of his solders. I went to his office to confront him. I had just gotten a promotion on my job, and I could see that my financial situation was better. I felt like this was the time to leave, or I never would. Well, as I was about to enter his office, I overheard him and someone in his office. As I opened the door, he was having sex with a woman on the floor behind his desk. I couldn't get angry. I felt relieved, and I had the strength that I didn't think I had. And I left, and we've been separated ever since. I filed for divorce immediately, and it is almost finalized. We have a lot of property tied up in it, so that's why it's been prolonged. But after he saw me and Stan one day walking on the beach, he confronted me and decided he will wait to sign off on the papers. I know I can get it done, but it will cost extra money to get a divorce without his signature, and he knows this. He had, he had..." She was getting out of breath, explaining so fast.

"Please stay calm. I'm not here to upset you. I want to make you comfortable and aware that you are not alone."

"Thanks, Elisa. Well, um, he came to the beach because I usually run three times a week on the beach. Well, this day, he decided to go check the mail. The doctor that I go to is a doctor we both go to, and he forgot to mail me my appointment at my new address, so that is how Mitchell realized I was pregnant, and he was so happy he came to the beach to confront me, but I was with Stan. Long story short, he came over after he realized Stan had left. He confronted me about the baby, wanted to know if it was his, and he decided to blackmail me into staying with him. He always wanted a baby. I just wouldn't give him one."

CAN'T STOP DESTINY

She started crying again. Elisa jumped up and hugged her tightly. As she calmed down, Carolyn felt the love that Elisa was giving her, and she looked up and gave her a smile.

"Girl, you sure you're just graduating? Because you have made me bring out things that no one could help me with. I feel so much better, but I just don't know what to do."

"Yes, you do, Carolyn. You are stronger than you know. You left. That's the first step, and you have grounds for divorce, adultery. No power can stop God. You have to tell Stan. Put your baby first even before Stan. My niece or nephew deserves you.

"Elisa, yes, you are so true. I thank you so much. I couldn't see for looking. I can't wait to tell Stan. He is going to be a great father. We really are a good team. I love your brother so much, and he loves me, I know. I just was so afraid."

"I really haven't been in your shoes, but I can only imagine your fears."

As they were talking, Stan was in his room, changing after taking a shower. He had hung up his clothes, and he put on a very sporty outfit; he loved the Ralph Lauren clothing line. He looked in the window, and as he looked back at himself, he thought about his baby, how he would love to dress him or her in the same outfits. He fell to the floor, crying. He looked up to heaven.

"God, I'm so sorry I made this baby outside your will. Father, I just want a chance to get it right. Please talk to Carolyn and let her know the baby is not a mistake. Please!" he cried out to God, which he hadn't done in a long time.

As he was getting up, wiping his face, the girls walked into the hotel room. He stared at Carolyn. He walked over and pulled her to him softly. She put her head in his chest.

"Baby, I love you. Carolyn, I need you and my child, but I love you enough to accept your decision. But the baby isn't—"

She interrupted him. "Stan, baby, I'm not killing our child, and I love you too. We can handle this together. Let's take a walk on the beach. I have a lot to explain."

Stan looked up, and he looked at Elisa. He walked over to his sister.

"My angel. What did you tell her, sis?"

"What she didn't tell me," Carolyn said, blushing. "She is a natural, Stan. She's going to earn that degree."

"Thanks, guys, but it's love for others and faith in God, goodness for all people. You know ever since our youth, Stan, seeing hurting people with Mom used to affect me. I just want to make a difference where and when I can. I am so happy for you both. Stan Junior, she's a winner. Anyone who's been through what she's been through and walked away to tell the story, God is with you. I can't wait to spoil my niece."

"Hey, who said it was a girl. My son is going to love you spoiling him."

"Well, I'll leave you two alone. I'm about to go get Rhonda. We have some shopping to do. I have a big day coming up next week. I hope to see you there, Carolyn," Elisa said as she walked over and hugged her.

CHAPTER 6

Shawn and Adam were now eight years old. *Time went by so fast,* Autumn, their mother, was thinking to herself as she was going to get the boys up for another one of Elisa's graduations. She was so proud of her kids. They had their storms, but they were not quitters.

"Adam, get up and come eat. We have a plane to catch."

She peeped in Adam's room. He was already up. She could hear him brushing his teeth. If she ever had to wake Adam, it was because he was asleep from studying all night, or he was sick.

"I hear you, Mom. I'm up already. I even said my prayers. I just was about to iron my slacks."

"Okay, that's a big boy. Why didn't you wake Shawn up?"

"I tried, Mommy. He wouldn't get up. He just hit at me, so I left him to you."

"You are so crazy. He's up. Let me go make sure I packed everything I need, and oh, did you both pack? Please tell me you are using the Polo luggage Stan bought? I don't want to have to hit your brother at the age of twenty-four and a half on the side of the head. He seriously needs to have his own son so he can stop making you both into little Stan Juniors and not Stan III. Well, let me take that back because Stan Junior got it from Stan Senior. I declare, if the man swag didn't turn me and half my school on, I wouldn't have been with him. It's hard buying for that man. That is why I give him gift cards."

"Really, Mommy? That's why your gifts are so small for holidays and birthdays. We thought you were giving him a card."

"No, silly. I love your dad. He is worth more than a card."

She kept laughing, walking out the door. As she entered her room, the phone rang, and she grabbed it, not wanting to answer, trying to get ready before Stan Senior was ready to go and be rushing her.

"Hello, Martin's residence."

"Hi, Mom. It's Stan, your handsome, sophisticated, strong, sexy, son."

"Is that all you have for me?"

"Yes, ma'am. I can't be telling all your son's secrets." They both laughed. "So, Mommy, what time will you be arriving in Tallahassee?"

"You sound like you're already there."

"Yes, ma'am, I am. And I have something important to share with you and Dad."

"Is it something I can wear or eat? Because if it's anything else, I don't want to hear. Let me know now so I can get prayed up."

"Ma, it's nothing you can eat or wear, but it's something you will love, hopefully sooner than later."

"Okay, okay, I trust that it's nothing I can't handle. You are a good son, and I think I raised you right. I mean you only caught I think ten whoopings your entire life."

"Yes, and I still manage to still be able to sit down. I think yours were the ones that kept me standing. Dad's hollering made me sit."

"Boy, you are crazy. We are leaving in a few. We are waiting on your dad. He had to go close some accounts before he leaves. He got off early so we could take the boys to their baseball game."

"Yes, that's what I'm talking about, keeping it in the family. My little brothers want to be like their brother, a baseball star."

"Yes, you're right, until the Air Force changed your mind. But I'm okay with it. You are getting a free education, and your rank is paying you the lifestyle your father wanted for you."

"What did you mean my father? What life did you want for your son, Mom?"

"I wanted you to have a life of love and peace. Don't get me wrong. I enjoy my life of finer things, but nothing can replace love

CAN'T STOP DESTINY

and strong foundation. I saw to it that you and your siblings got it. Your father's upbringing was good, but he didn't have a silver spoon like I did, so he thought money first, then family. This meant long nights at work, leaving you and your sister being with me when I work, at home, in the stores, etc. Wherever I was, I was not letting money and people raise my children, but your father is a great provider. He showed you guys love every time possible. He made sure you all knew you had a dad that cares and loves you, so it balanced itself out."

"It did, Mommy. I remember those long nights, especially when I had baseball and track meets. But when he showed up to my games, everybody knew he was there and that he was my father. So I appreciate you both how you kept us close, and I know the twins are being blessed also."

"Yes, they are. In fact, since his business is more established, he can take them to practice and go to all their games. I'm thankful he is making up for what he couldn't give you. Because Elisa was under me at work all the time, that's why she is a doctor. I remember when she accidentally heard one of my social sessions. When I came out of the room, she was crying so hard. She was about eleven or twelve. She ran into my arms. She said, 'Mommy I'm going to be a doctor that help people who can't help themselves think.' I smiled because what happened was my patient was going through a mental breakdown, and they wanted to put her in a psychiatric ward, but they needed my approval. The lady was pouring out her heart and feelings to me, and I realized she was not crazy. She just needed love and, mostly, financial assistance for her and her children. She was a single mother, and she lost her job. And her husband had passed three months previously. So you guys staying connected too, maybe my grandchildren too will have a blessed life like you all."

Stan got quiet because his surprise was just that, and he didn't know how she would handle it, not the pregnancy but that it's out of marriage to a married woman whom he also just became engaged to.

As their parents drove up in a 2009 Bentley they had rented from the airport, Stan Junior walked out to greet them. He started blushing, seeing that his father was still the suave man he probably would always be. His mother complained, but when she got out of the car, she was wearing Versace from head to toe, red and black pantsuit with black shoes and jewels to enhance it, and that Prada purse just put the icing on the cake.

Elisa dressed just like her, but she would buy her a wardrobe, and she would wear it until the next line came in. She didn't believe in throwing money around, even though her life savings was good enough to do it with. Their father gave it to her as soon as she reached twenty and a half, just before her twenty-first birthday that would be coming up in five months.

The twins were so handsome. Even at eight, you couldn't tell them apart, but fate fixed that with their different complexions. Of course, they had their Polo matching outfits on. Adam must have picked it for them because Shawn would have worn his Levi's jeans with a T-shirt and been just as happy.

Stan Junior walked up to his mother and kissed her on the lips and gave her a strong hug. He faked his father and gave him a kiss on the chick and gave him a strong sideways hug. His father taught him that when he became a teenager. You hug a man by grabbing his hand and hugging him sideways. He said it's a man thing.

"Hi, little buddies." He picked one up, and then he tried to grab the other one.

But he said, "Hey! I'm not a baby anymore, man!" Shawn put his hand out to be shaken.

"You know what, buddy, you're right." Stan Junior laughed, then he grabbed him anyway.

"You will never be old as me, little man."

"So where is our graduate?" his parents asked at the same time, sounding like proud parents.

"She is in the shower. She doesn't even know you are here yet. Wait until she sees you sitting in her living room."

Elisa was listening to Najee, one of her favorite jazz singers. She looked in the mirror and started talking to herself. "Okay, Elisa you are not there yet. Stay focused. You have come close to the finish line. But this is just another pole you must jump over. Now we have to get the business off because, girl, you know people are counting on you.

CAN'T STOP DESTINY

And you look good, if I can say so, in your Dolce & Gabbana dress. Two, three more wears, and you will be a blessing for the shelter ladies. Man, you look good, girl."

She busted out laughing.

"Okay, Elisa, you're starting to sound like your patients."

She began laughing again. As she was trying to zip the dress, her mother walked in.

"So do you need some help, or is the person you're talking to in that mirror going to help you?"

"Mommy!" She ran into her arms. "Mommy, when did you guys get here? I didn't hear a doorbell. Even though you have keys, I know you. You will still ring the bell."

"Yes, that's called respect. You are a woman now, even though I hope you wait for your husband, but you know this new generation."

"Ma'am, I'm a good girl, even though my womanhood sometimes itches."

They both laughed so loud her father came up to check on them.

"Can I enter please?"

Elisa ran to the door.

"Yes, Dad."

She jumped into his arms like she was still that little girl that went to school on the first day of school. She could still remember it. Her father was pressing for time, but Elisa said she needed him on the first day. As her parents walked her into her school, she looked at all the kids, and she grabbed her father around the legs. As her mother was signing the paperwork, he picked her up, and she held him so tight. He was scared to leave her. As the teacher walked up to him, she gave him a trusting look. And he put her down at her desk, and as she saw other kids sitting like big girls, she looked up at her father. She said, "I'm a big girl too, Dad."

"I came in to check on you two. You sound like I had to come hurt somebody."

"No, sir. Inside joke, Dad. I'm glad you made it safe. So what kind of car you rented this time? Don't tell me a Bentley."

"You know Dad has to ride in the finer things. I wouldn't be Dad if I drove in anything less—"

PAMELA GREEN

"You know what, honey," his wife interrupted, "I'm going to rent a Ford Focus next time and save that money and go shopping."

"Baby, my employees don't drive that 'found on the rode' dead cars. All my company cars are SUVs—Cadillac Escalades," her dad said as they all laughed.

Stan walked in with the twins. "Here we go. Dad must be bragging about his company again."

"No, your mother is trying to insult me for being me."

"Stan, I love you, but sometimes you are too conceited. But you back it up with your love, so I'm sorry," she said, kissing him romantically in front of their kids.

"Aw!" the twins said at the same time.

"Go to your rooms down the hall please. It's my day, so please let anything else wait until tonight, parents," Elisa joked.

As they arrived at the stadium, they saw the graduates lining up, and Elisa was in the top five. Her parents were so proud of her. As they sat down together, Elisa waved at them from the front line. As she was marching, she was thinking of William Harris and how he was at her high school graduation and what he had told her. She blushed as if he was standing up there waiting for her and wishing he was, but he wasn't. And she hadn't heard about him since her mother told her he moved to France to teach.

CHAPTER 7

"Good morning, sir," the waitress said in French.

"Good morning," he replied in French.

"How can I assist you on this great morning?"

"I will take some French coffee for one. You get it? French coffee."

"Yes, sir," the waitress smiled, not finding the joke funny, but he was so handsome saying it she laughed anyway. "So, sir, would you like the special?"

"No, I will take some buttery grits, two sausage patties, and toast to dip in my coffee."

"To dip your coffee in, sir?" the waitress asked, looking confused.

William looked at the confusion in her face and blushed.

"Well, growing up, my grandfather would take his bread and dip it in his coffee, and he taught me to do it, so I've been doing it ever since. You try it. You might really like it."

"Well, sir, I've never heard of it. Might just try it on my next break."

"Well, if I'm not here, I hope you enjoy my coffee-and-bread recipe."

They both laughed as she went off to take care of his order. As he was reading the magazine, he saw an ad on the graduates in high schools and colleges, and he thought of Elisa.

I wonder if she is graduating this year? William pondered. *She is so driven. I'm sure she is.* He then remembered what he had told her, and since he would be almost through with his teaching, he was thinking of going back to the States for a small break. But then he thought to himself, *She wouldn't want an old man like me now, twenty-six years old.* He started staring into space, wondering if he should get in touch with her and how he couldn't keep her off his mind. *Man, you got it bad.* "Man, I need to move on. I'm sure she has."

"Yes, man, you need to move on," Sam, his friend and coworker for the last three years, said.

"Sam, you shouldn't interrupt a man when he is holding a conversation by himself. I heard it could be dangerous."

"Yes, I'm sure it can but, man, I've known you for about three years now. I know you probably had some at least three times in the last three years. These women are throwing themselves at you. And you just push them away. What does that woman have down there? Real gold? If so, can you go back to the States and get me some to spend? My rent and light bill is due."

"Hey, man, you're wrong for that, and I don't know if she has gold down there. I never had it."

"What! Come on, my friend, you got to be joking."

"No, I'm not. In fact, I barely kissed her."

"What? You never touched the gold?"

"Never. I was her teacher, and she was my student. We are about five and a half years apart."

"What? You fell in love with one of your students? My friend, tell me it isn't so!"

"Sam, man, it's not like that. You know I graduated out of college at a young age. I was twenty-one when I was teaching her, and this woman is so different than most women I know her age. She graduated a year early too. We used to tutor my students together. She ran my errands, and she got me out of so many deadlines with printing, filing, computer work, man. And to top that off, she is so beautiful, and her spirit matches her looks."

CAN'T STOP DESTINY

"Her spirit, man. You fell in love with your student, and that is a carnal rule. *Never, never, ever* fall in love with your students."

"Who said I was in love with her?"

"William, you have been away from her going on four years. You've been out of the States for three years. You are a good teacher and all, but you are into your work so heavy you barely date, unless I drag you out. And you only get booty if the girls almost have to rape you. Sounds like love to me, man."

William paused and looked at his breakfast coming, but he just looked at the waitress.

"Sir, sir, your food, sir," the waitress said in French. He replied in English, thinking so hard he forgot where he was. "Sir?" she said, not quite understanding him.

"Sorry," Sam said in French. "He is in la-la land. Snap out of it, William."

"Oh, sorry," he said in French. "Thanks, it looks grand."

"Well, don't dip your bread too much, sir," she joked, making Sam look confused.

"Inside joke, Sam. You had to be there," William said, smiling as she walked away.

"Anyway, man, I got your message. You are thinking about going to the States on our summer break."

"Yes, man. You want to go with me? I haven't been home in a long time. It's almost a year since I last went home to check on my condo and make sure my brother isn't destroying it."

"I don't know why you kept it. I would have sold it myself."

"Well, I'm buying it, and it's not just a condo man. It's on the beachfront. It's a good investment. I might put my brother out and start leasing it out for people on vacations, etc. I'm really thinking of it."

"Well, that sounds like a winner. So you want me to go to the States with you, hmm?

"Man, all you have to spend is airfare. You can stay at my house. And just think about it. You will have all those half-naked women running on the beach, with waves roaring and beautiful sunsets."

"Man, you can stop trying. You had me at women running half naked. I'm so in. So when do we leave?"

"Well, I will reserve my plane ticket for Sunday, and I'll just book yours with mine. I won't be teaching this summer, so I probably won't be back until fall semester."

"I'm not either, so are you okay with me staying with you in your crib that long?"

"As long as you respect it and me. I like a clean house, and if you bring a woman over, keep her in line. Feel me?"

"Oh yes, I feel you, bro. And what about the love of your life? What's her name again?"

"Elisa, and I didn't tell you that."

"I know, but just in case, I want to meet the angel that touched my buddy."

"You probably won't meet her man. She is living in Tallahassee, Florida. That's where she went to college. But I think she is graduating this year I don't know if she's moving back to Pensacola or what."

"Or what, man? You need to find out, and you need to at least say hello. She's a woman now. You might get lucky, my friend."

"Man, is that all you think about? Is sex on the brain?"

"No! Man, I think about a good hot homemade meal with a woman butt naked cooking it."

"Sam, let's go." William laughed at his friend. "Man, you almost messed up my meal, but I'm hungry."

"William, man, why'd you keep putting that bread in your coffee?"

"Man, long story. I will tell you one day. But right now, I need to open my computer and get our flights together. I won't need to rent a car. My car is at my house, locked up in my garage. I didn't let my brother touch my baby."

"So what are you driving, William?"

"I'm driving a dark-black Porsche 2006, off the showroom floor, limited, with all the features—with leather seats, black also."

"Man, you left that car for three years!"

"Yes, but when I went home, I drove it. I haven't been home this last year. You and I know why. Between teaching and my side business teaching students how to make their own computers, it will keep you busy. But this year, I'm going to see about my baby."

"Which one, Elisa or the Porsche?" Sam teased.

William paused and said in his head, *Both*.

CHAPTER 8

As her parents were setting up to go to dinner with Elisa and some of her classmates and their parents, Autumn started wondering what it was that Stan Junior wanted to tell her that he wanted to wait until after this important day of Elisa. It made Autumn wonder, but she just hoped the Lord would prepare her for whatever it was because even though Stan Junior was her most challenging child outside of Shawn—she blushed—he was a good older son.

"So why am I worrying?" she spoke out to herself. "I better stop before I need to be Elisa's first patient."

"So what restaurant will we be meeting your friends at?" Stan Junior asked Elisa while she was fixing the family some smoothies to start the evening with.

"Well, it's kind of pricey, but the food and the ambiance and services are perfect. It's a steak-and-seafood restaurant. The owner's name was given to me by one of my teachers that took us there after one of our biggest finals. Bro, it will be worth the money. It's Shula's 346 Grill. You will be blessed. Try the cheesecake or carrot cake, and of course, they are famous for it. And there's wine also. It's my day. I will drink at least one or two."

"Well, sis, after all that hard work, you are worth the money. In fact, dinner is on me, and I have a surprise to tell you before I tell our parents because you are the reason I have the surprise. But you can't tell no one until I do. Pinky promise?"

CAN'T STOP DESTINY

"I promise, pinky promise. So come on out with it!"

"Well, I asked Carolyn to marry me as soon as her divorce is finalized, and she accepted."

"What! Really? I'm so happy for you both."

Elisa and Stan paused, acting like twins but not.

"Mom!" they said at the same time.

"Yes, Mommy. I know. But I will tell her tomorrow, her and dad. But I don't know if I should tell them together or apart."

"Well, big brother, it's like this dad going trip because it might be a threat to your money." They both laughed. "But, Mother—oh my god, she's not only pregnant. She is married and, to top that off, to your boss. It seems scandalous and premeditated, but we both know it isn't, but at first, she will see it that way. So you know what, either way, she will have to get used to the deal. It's your life, and last I check, Mommy doesn't put your pants on. She doesn't pay for that loft you live in. She doesn't pay for that Mercedes you drive. You get the point."

"Yes, I do, sis, I do. Man, you need to stay out of the doctor mode for a while. You could stop at I'm grown."

They both laughed so hard Elisa had tears coming out from laughing so hard.

"Okay, what is the joke?"

Their parents asked, walking down the hallway after admiring the setup which was real classy, like a hotel setup, that Autumn set up for her daughter. Elisa had a two-bedroom apartment that she shared with a college classmate who, after a while, was always late with her share of the payments. She decided to keep it and stay by herself the last two years of college. Her father was afraid for her at first, but her mother convinced him that if he let her go to college away from them, he could trust God to complete what he was starting in their daughter. So he not only supported her; he put up the deposit and the first month's rent. After that, she paid her own bills with her job and her allowance her father gave her all through college.

"Nothing, Mother. Elisa is trying to tell me about my dressing. She said I should be tired of Ralph Lauren after eight years—all through high school and college and now the service. But I'm not.

PAMELA GREEN

I'm a Polo man. It was made for me, and that's how it's going to stay. Right, buddies?" he said, rubbing the twins on the head that had it on from top to the bottom just like their big brother.

"You know this, big bro," Adam said. He also loved the line, and Shawn did whatever they asked of him.

"Well, I don't know about you, guys?" Stan Senior said, walking toward the bar in her kitchen. "I'm about to enjoy this smoothie, and I'm ready to go get me some food."

As they all entered the restaurant, they gave the keys to the valet parkers.

"Sir, I will take good care of your Bentley," they said, happy to drive it. The men did paper-scissors on who would park it.

"Well, young men, if I were in your position, I would do the same. It's a Bentley all right, for God's sake. Keep working hard, taking steps higher and higher, and you will have your own one day. This is a rental, sons, but mine is at home in my garage. Can't put all those miles on my Missy. That's her name, Missy Blue, because she is dark blue with peanut-butter leather seats. I bought her cash. You want know how?"

"Yes, sir." He had their undivided attention.

"Well, in my college years, I started paying myself car notes, putting it in an account that drew interest. And I drove a Lincoln Town Car that I paid cash for working part time after school. I took care of it, and I drove it all my college years. And about six years after I finished college, I had paid enough to go get me a 1989 Bentley. It still drives like a baby. It's my dream car, so when I travel, I always rent one. God, prayer, and suffering got me this Bentley, sons."

"Man," they said at the same time, "sounds like a plan, sir."

The one that won got in the car, put on his seat belt, and felt like a million dollars.

"Dad, can you come on? We've heard that story all our lives!" they joked.

"Yes, you did, and Ms. Elisa, you got this far listening to your old dad. Lemonade businesswoman." He laughed, and they all laughed walking into the restaurant.

"Hi, thought you guys weren't going to ever make it!"

80

CAN'T STOP DESTINY

Elisa screamed. It was her best friend Rhonda who thought she wasn't going to be able to make the occasion, but her boss gave her time off earlier for her friend. They all were greeting each other as the hostess was getting their reserved seating together. Elisa and Rhonda were holding hands like they were still in elementary.

"Girls, I pray your kids be just as close as you both have been since elementary," Autumn said, kissing them both on the forehead.

"Well, I thank God for my baby girl but always felt like I had two daughters," Stan Senior said.

As they were being escorted to be seated, they all were noticing the beauty of the establishment.

"Man, Elisa, this is nice!" Stan Junior said, stopping at the bar as they were showing them to their seats. "I might come back here with my lady friend."

They both laughed and went to meet the others.

The next morning, the birds were chirping so loud Elisa got up and looked at her clock and got up to prepare everyone breakfast. It was a long night of laughter and some tears, of parents telling about the long hauls of their kids and the battles yet to come. It was nine in the morning. She walked in the living room, seeing everyone sleeping where they could. One of the twins was on the floor, one on the twin couch, and Stan Junior was on her big sofa with a blanket over his face. She walked into the kitchen that was separated from the living room by her bar with hanging wine glasses and four bar stools made by one of her favorite designers, Renzo Faucigilietti. The adjustable stool design is within reach. The price was worth it. She had said, "It will be good in my home." She started the coffee. Out of all coffees, she loved Community, and the smell went all through the apartment.

"Okay, what can I fix these people after all that good food? I might wait until they get up. I hate to waste my money. Besides, the twins always want cereal. I bought at least three boxes for them. I might just wait," she said, talking to herself like she always does. "I guess living alone makes you talk to yourself a lot." She laughed aloud, grabbing her mouth, not wanting to wake anyone up.

"Girl, are you sure you don't need a doctor?" Stan Junior said, walking into the kitchen.

PAMELA GREEN

"No," she whispered. "Good morning, big bro. This is the big day. Are you ready to break the news to your parents?"

"No, I'm not, and why are you whispering?"

"I don't want to wake them up."

"Oh, you are right because I'm not ready for the drama."

"So how are the baby to be and Carolyn?"

"She is doing great. We talked all night, until she started getting sleepy and had nausea."

"Nausea, now it sounds real. It hasn't hit me. I'm going to be an aunt. Stan Junior, you are going be a father. I am so looking forward to the future. You know she's going be spoiled, the next girl since me."

"Well, I didn't think of it that way. We have a lot of knuckleheads. Well, since I love you so much, I will pray and ask God for a daughter."

"Yes, and we will name her Alisha, like Elisa."

"Okay, now you are forgetting that she has a mother, but since you saved her life, we have to include you some kind of way. Sis, I really still thank you for your love and patience for others."

"No, I thank you for trusting me with your future life. You actually put your trust in my education."

"Yes, ma'am. Elisa, you are the most driven woman I've ever met since Stan Senior."

"Oh, now I'm compared to dad. Where does that leave me? At least Dad won't die alone."

"Alone—you'll never be alone, Elisa. Beautiful as you are, God has someone for you. Just stay you, little sis. Hey, what happened to that man you told me you cared about three years ago? I know Troy has been trying to sneak back. But, little sis, for you to stay single for so long, you must really care about that fellow."

Elisa got quiet. She turned, and to keep from feeling what her heart had been feeling, she held the tear in and drank a sip of her coffee.

"You, all right, little sis? I didn't mean to bring up old feelings."

"I'm all right. You know, William isn't just another man. He is very different than any man I had met, and when he walked into my

82

CAN'T STOP DESTINY

life five and a half years ago, my life hasn't been the same. We had a connection that we both couldn't explain or admit to one another because of our age difference."

"How much older is he, sis, than you again?"

"Well, he should be twenty-five and a half now. Our birthdays are actually a month apart. But I haven't heard from him. But Mommy's friend said he was going to Paris to teach."

"Man, you ran the man away!" he said, trying to make her smile.

She turned and smiled. As she turned, her friend Rhonda came in. She slept with her last night instead of driving all the way back to Pensacola.

"Hey, guys. You all right? It feels heavy in here. And good morning?"

"We're all right," Stan said, hugging his little sister and walking off to make himself a cup of coffee.

"Hey, I take a cup, three sugars and little cream."

"Rhonda, one cup coming up," Stan said as she sat at the bar area.

As they were sitting, drinking coffee, their father came down the hall.

"Good morning, my family. I slept good, baby girl, in that full bed. Your mother might be on the floor."

"Dad, did you put my mother on the floor?" Elisa said, sounding worried.

He and Stan Junior started laughing.

"Baby, I'm just joking. Your mother is coming. She was too tired to take a shower last night. And where did you find that restaurant? I'm going to have my company party there this Christmas."

"Thanks, Dad. It was a restaurant one of my professors turned us on to when she took us there after a hard finale."

"We couldn't stop talking about it last night, your mother and I. And you know I love a little class in my life."

"Little, Dad!" Stan Junior said, almost spitting his coffee out.

"Dad, you're the reason I wear only Polo or the next-in-line designers because, you know, Ralph Lauren is my man. But you're the reason I rent Bentleys and drive a Mercedes, live in a high-rise loft. I'm going to college for computer science while getting paid by the air force."

"Okay, okay, I get the point!"

"Well, I can go on, Dad. I didn't even start with that house you live in and my sister here, who is starting her own business in one month. Shall I go on or stop?"

"Please stop," their mother said as she walked in, in the middle of the conversation. "Yes, your son is right. You love more than a little class. Good morning, everyone."

"Where are the boys at?"

"Good morning, Mommy," Elisa said, kissing her mother on the cheek. "Do you want a cup of Community coffee? And are the twins still asleep in the living room?"

"Oh, my poor babies. They were trying to hang with us grown-ups."

"So, Stan Junior, what is the news that I had to wait a whole day for?"

"Okay, I think I need another cup of coffee?" Rhonda said, being nosy and ready to hear.

"So Rhonda knows before me, Stan Junior?"

"Rhonda," Stan said, looking at her as if to say "you need to be cool please." He looked at his mother and did a big sigh.

"Well, I'm waiting to hear too," Stan Senior was sipping his coffee and reading the newspaper with one eye up and one eye down. "Your mother is already trying to worry me, asking me all night what it could be, what it could be," he repeated, making a joke out of it.

"Baby, it's not funny," Autumn said, looking at Stan Junior, concerned.

"Son, can you take your mother out of her misery? Please, son?"

"Yes, sir. Well, Mommy, it's like this…um…I'm going to be a father, and I'm getting married as soon as my baby's mother gets a divorce."

His mother sat down at the kitchen table and sipped her coffee. She didn't say a word.

"Son, she's married. How'd you let this happen?"

"Well, while I'm confessing, let me tell you everything because I know you will find out eventually. She is married to my boss."

CAN'T STOP DESTINY

"Okay, son, now that is really calling on a death wish. You worked too hard. You've been working for the air force seven and a half years! You can't mess up your future, son. But what about this marriage, divorce?" His father's voice kept rising.

"Mom, what do you have to say?" Stan Junior asked, looking worried about her the most.

"Stan, I raised you better than this. How could you let that woman set you up like this? To top it off, she is bringing a baby in the middle of this, and will you be losing your job, son, behind this?"

"No, Ma. I got transferred, and it's not the way it sounds," Stan Junior said, as calmly as possible. He hated it when his mother gets upset, and he always never raised his voice to her.

"Son, it's just how it sounds!" His mother raised her voice, waking up the twins.

"Hey, man, what's the shouting about!"

Adam said, walking in the kitchen, grabbing a bowl for cereal. Shawn went straight to the bathroom. He didn't even care about the noise.

"Adam, can you go into the room down the hall please and make Shawn cereal and take them with you? This is grown-ups talk, baby. I'll call you out when we're through."

"Stan, she sounds as if she set you up, son!" his mother said, trying to keep her cool.

"Mother, she did not set me up. We met at a restaurant one night. We hit it off. She was already separated, and she had already filed for divorce. I knew she was married, but she didn't know that her husband was my boss. He told her after her doctor sent her test results to the wrong address. She used the same doctor that her husband and her had for her insurance. She gave him her new address, but the doctor forgot and mailed her results to her husband. And he came to confront her and saw me and her together on the beach. He confronted her and let her know that I was one of his best employees and that he was going to make it hard for me. But I went over his head, pulled some strings, and he is no longer my boss. I asked Carolyn to marry me."

"Carolyn is her name," Stan Senior retorted.

85

"Okay, so how do you know this wasn't a part of her plan, son?" both his parents screamed at the same time.

"Mother, Dad!" Elisa screamed over them. "He is not lying. It isn't all black and white. It isn't like it looks!"

"So you knew all this time, young lady, and you didn't say anything?" Her mother started crying. "I just want the best for my children. How could you betray me this way?"

"Mommy, he didn't betray you and Dad. This is his life. Did you forget he is grown, Mother? I know she is telling the truth because Stan Junior came to me a week ago, all upset because Carolyn was going to have an abortion, until I went to Miami to convince her not to. Mom, I heard the whole story. She was being mentally abused by this man. And she had the power to walk. But he was going to use the baby and Stan to break the courage she had built up to leave him. And when she tried to confront him, he was sleeping with another woman in his office on the floor. Mommy, I know it sounds like something out of a soap, but it is true, and your son needs his parents' love, not criticism. He needs that strength you and Dad put in us to be used by you both, please! It's your grandchild. Would you rather they killed the baby and Stan Junior go on with his life?"

Autumn got quiet. Stan Senior walked over to his son and pulled him to him, and it wasn't a sideways hug like most men do. He hugged his son close to let him know he really cared.

"Son, I'm sorry. I should have known better. I am proud that you want to make this woman, I mean Carolyn, an honest woman. And, son, you are my oldest, and you are giving me my first grandson. Thank you."

He kissed his son on the forehead.

"Grandson," Autumn said, walking to her son and kissing him. She hugged him tight and started talking through her tears. "I need another girl. Elisa is sweet and all, but she's older now and a doctor. She doesn't need me anymore. I need me another intelligent daughter."

"Oh, Mommy, I'm still your little girl, and I will always be. No baby can take my spot, but she sure will come close."

While they all stood hugging, Rhonda ran over. "Oh, I'm so happy, but I feel left out though."

CAN'T STOP DESTINY

"Come on, Rhonda. I can't believe you didn't tell me," Autumn joked.

"Oh no, ma'am, you're not going to make Stan Junior and Elisa stop taking me on trips to Miami. The next trip might be Paris!" she joked.

Elisa looked at her and blushed and said in her mind, *She might just get her wish.*

CHAPTER 9

As William entered the airport, he couldn't help but think of Elisa, how close he was to her than hours ago when he was in Paris, France. As the people were talking over the loud mike, it felt strange. He was so used to listen for two languages; he felt left out. He busted out laughing at how he must look as if he was feeling strange, even weird.

"Man, William, Florida is so beautiful man. I know we needed a change," Sam joked. "But if I lived in Florida, I wouldn't have gone to Paris. But hey, when you're smart and you apply and you get out of the country, and I mean country South Texas, you want to get as far as you can. When the job offer was available, I jumped on it. No wife, no children—what's to keep me there? My mother passed, and my father started over with my stepmother and siblings. I was good to go, man, so I did."

"Man, Sam, I heard that story before, but every time I hear it, man, I respect you even the more. If I didn't have my parents, I don't know how I would have turned out. You must have a great father and stepmother."

"I do, man. They were a little strict. I was the oldest, so they made me an example, but they made sure I had the best education, and that I am thankful for. My stepmother, whom I call mommy, calls me every other day to make sure I'm okay. I guess I'll go home for one of these weekends, and you can go to the country with me if you want, man?"

88

CAN'T STOP DESTINY

"I just might do that. Why not? You seem to be trustworthy. I guess you won't let the animals eat me alive, at least I hope."

They both started laughing, and as the cab drove up closer, William gave him his address. As they were about to enter the cab, some ladies screamed at them, asking for their numbers.

"All right, a Florida welcome!" Sam said, ready to flirt.

"No, sir, we have to go. I need to relax and shower, and besides, I arrived sooner than I told my brother. I want to catch him off guard in my house, man."

"There you go again, William. You're always cunt blocking!"

"Cunt blocking, I thought it was called cock blocking." They both got in, laughing hysterically as Sam waved bye to the ladies.

"Man, William, this lady, the love of your life, she better be worth me not getting mine."

"Man, I didn't say I was here for her. I am here on vacation at home, from home. And if I see Elisa, and that's a big if, I will be very appreciative just to see a great student."

"So you are still trying to convince yourself she is just a good, oh, I mean great, student." Sam laughed. "Okay, my friend. I can't wait to meet this woman."

"Here we are, sir," the cab driver said, laughing at Sam. "Need help with your luggage?"

"No, thank you. Two men better be able to tote their own luggage."

William gave him the fee and a ten-dollar tip.

"Thanks!" the cab driver said, smiling as he drove off.

As William entered his home, he looked around. He loved hearing the ocean beating up against his back fence. He walked upstairs to see if his brother was in yet. As he looked at his surroundings, he was surprised to see that his home was still standing. He walked over and turned his CD player on with built-in stereo sound that went all around. Sam jumped and could not believe how smooth his friend's condo sounded.

"Man, William, for a man that doesn't like getting laid often, you sure have this place ready for nothing but it."

"Sam, I like getting laid man. I just don't like laying with dogs. I don't want to get up with fleas. And besides, I had plans, and women are just distractions that I didn't need at the time."

"And you are established now, William. You have two places—one in the country, one out of the country—a job to die for, your own business, and now all you need is the love of your life, right, man? Elisa."

"You said that, not me. I need to take one day at a time."

"Man, you need to get out of that book you are living in and come to the real world. You have a life that most men dream of."

"Sam, I'm going to call in some food, and I'm going to sit on my couch and watch a good movie that I'm going to enjoy now, my friend. Your bedroom is down that hall on the end. You have to share the bathroom with my brother, but I checked, and it's still usable. I hope my brother is still alive, man. He is twenty-two, but man, he has actually proved me wrong about him."

"William, I guess he is more like you than you thought."

"Well, he is in college to be an engineer. It's his third year. I moved him in here because he didn't like campus life. My parents told me they would keep an eye on him, and so far, he only had one big party that almost got out of hand, and that was about two years ago. My father handled it. He is a sergeant in the Miami investigation department, so when they saw that badge and he stands five ten and he lives in the gym…may I say anymore, man?"

"No, sir, I would have got on the straight and narrow too if he walked in the party I was in. Do I want to meet him, man?"

"Man, he is the humblest man I know. Now my mother is the one you need to run from. She is a lawyer, and she is one of the best in her field, man—criminal lawyer. That's how they met. He was handling one of her customers, and one thing led to me and my little brother."

"Okay, William, I've heard enough before I get on the next plane to Texas, missing my family. I'm going to take a shower, get comfortable, and hit that beach."

"Hope a hurricane don't come," William joked.

"Come on, man. You had me at your mother. Don't scare me anymore."

CAN'T STOP DESTINY

Sam walked in the room, and he couldn't believe the room. It had a flat screen on the wall, vaulted ceiling with sunroof windows, a dark-red oak desk, leather cushion seats, with a computer, color printer, and fax machine. There was a red reclining seat, a full-size colonial bed with furniture to match. The closet was walk-in, big enough for a small mini car to fit in.

"Man, this is the life. I might just move in with your brother," Sam joked.

William walked upstairs to his room. As he walked in, he fell on the twin black-leather Italian sofa he put in his room that he had since college. It was still looking as good as when his mother bought it his last year in college. As he lay down, he looked out the window that covered one end of the wall to the next. The ocean waves were beating against the backyard fence. He loved seeing the ocean, and he couldn't wait for the sunset. He forgot about Pensacola sunsets. *What a sight*, he said in his mind.

CHAPTER 10

As Stan Junior walked in the living room, his phone went off. It was the love of his life, Carolyn. He was waiting for his mother and Elisa to come back from Florida State University. She had some last-minute things to take care of. So while they were there, his father and Stan Junior were waiting to go to Lake Ella Park. They might as well make it a family vacation before Stan Junior went back to Miami. The family agreed.

"Hello, baby, how are you doing?" Stan Junior asked, happy to hear her voice.

"Hi, love. I'm going for my doctor's visit, and the next one, you have to be there. I'll get to see her for the first time."

"You mean him, right? You forgot we are going to have a son, unless you are having twins."

"Please, Stan. Don't do this to me. Are you trying to lose all of this beautiful shape you fell in love with? Besides, how can I name her Autumn if she's a he?"

"Baby, you are going to name her after my mother? You do love me!"

"Yes, I do, love. So can you agree it's a little Autumn?"

"Yes. So I'm glad you fell in love with my mother just by talking to her over the phone."

"She was so nice, and she was so understanding. And she is planning to come to Miami soon. She actually wants to be at one of

CAN'T STOP DESTINY

the baby visits. And she wants us to go to dinner alone so we can get more acquainted."

"You aren't nervous at all, are you? When I met your parents, I was so afraid, Carolyn. Are you trying to tell me you weren't just a little afraid?"

"No, baby. For one thing, I was just telling them about my divorce and you in the same sentence. And thank God my parents already knew how abusive he was. You were just a scaredy cat."

"Yes, baby, I was a little afraid. No, I was a lot afraid!" They both busted out laughing.

"Stan baby, I can't wait to see you, but enjoy your family. I'll see you tomorrow night."

As Elisa walked up to the waterfall at Florida State University, she touched it, thinking about the many years she walked up the stairs.

She asked herself, *Should I go up the middle row or the first row or the second row of stairs? Well, since it's my last year, I will walk up the last row of stairs.* As she looked at the burgundy and black one more time, she walked down the hall. She saw her mother coming up to her.

"Elisa, how do you guys climb these stairs every day?"

Elisa smiled. "Well, Mommy, I don't climb them every day. Thank God I've been doing my clinical the last year since I went to the college of medicine. I came to this campus just to take care of school needs and when I did my work studies. You know I've been working full time off campus also."

"So have you decided when you are going to pack all your things and move back home?" her mother said, trying not to sound excited.

"Mom, I know you are excited. Why you are pretending?"

"Yes, I am. My baby is moving back to Pensacola. I am happy, and I'm so proud of you, baby. I talked to my friend Susan, and she is still looking for the property you asked for. You say you are not like your father, but you sure are picky about where you want to live."

"Mom, I'm not picky. I just want what I like, and I work hard to get it."

"Yes, you do, and you work so hard I wonder if I will ever get my future son-in-law and grandchildren."

"Whoa, grandchildren. Mother, slow down. I haven't got to that part yet. I'm just getting my business started."

"Okay, okay, young woman. I will pray for God to give me patience with my daughter, the career-minded lady. Oh, before I forget, I talked to one of your classmates. She said she went to Paris for winter break. She is majoring in fashion design, and she said she ran into Mr. Harris and that he is teaching at the university she attended and this is her last year. She said he is as gorgeous as he was when he taught you both."

As her mother was talking, Elisa felt like the world had stopped, and she heard her mother, but she sounded like her voice was fading.

"Ma, hmm," she said, trying to focus on what to say next.

"Did you hear me?" she said. "She saw your closest teacher. Mr. William was his name, right?"

"Yes, Ma. How did she say he was doing?"

"She said he didn't get to see her. She saw him on passing the day before she was about to leave. She said she tried to get to him, but she had to go before she missed her plane. And one of her classmates that flew back with her told her she took his class, and she couldn't concentrate on learning for looking at him. Man, I tell you, he was a catcher. Your father would have had a run for his money if he was going to school with me."

"Mommy, he was my teacher," Elisa said, blushing inside.

"I know, but you two were so close, those late nights and all. I'm sure you felt something, young lady. You tell me later."

Elisa looked at her mother and thought to herself, *If she only knew how much I was crazy about that man.*

"Mommy, I'm thinking of taking a trip to Paris after I get my business off the floor. Maybe I'll see your little boyfriend and tell him how you feel so Dad can break his and your neck."

"Elisa, I would enjoy the breakage after being with that hunk."

"Mommy, you are a married woman."

"Yes, I am, but I'm not dead. I'm just faithful. He would make a good catch, and he is not that older than you. Maybe you are to look him up. I'm just saying."

CAN'T STOP DESTINY

"Let's go, Mom. The lake is calling my name. I need the down-time anyway, and the twins are going to love it," she said, changing the subject.

CHAPTER 11

As William was waking up from his nap, he saw the sunset that he was waiting for since he had been gone. The sun made the beach in his back window look like fire was in it, mixed with yellow in the water. He could see couples walking as he lifted up his bathroom window which showed the front of the beach. He had a beach home that centered on the corner of the beach to the front of the beach which would be a big property sale if he ever decided to sell. He got the property six years ago when the area was not as upgraded as it was now for the tourist attractions along the beach. He got in the shower and changed. As he walked down into his living room, he noticed that his brother had made it in.

"Hey, sleepyhead," his brother said as he gave him a tight hug. "Man, I thought you were dead. I met your friend. He's cool, man. He's getting dressed. He met a few honeys. He's inviting us to go out and eat with them."

"No, thanks, little bro. And I'm glad to see you took care of the place. I'm about to go see about my baby though, then I'll give you the rest of your props."

"Man, your car has been chilling since you left. It only left the time you asked Dad to go get your inspection stickers updated. Man, you need a woman. You come all the way here just to see about a car and a house."

CAN'T STOP DESTINY

"No, man. I came back to see my hometown and the people I left here and enjoy some of Pensacola sunrises and sunsets."

"Don't tell me you're ready to move back home. I'm enjoying your crib, big bro, and it keeps me getting the honeys, if you know what I mean."

"Yes, I do, and how are you doing in your studies? Mom told me you've been doing well. Don't let them women distract you. You are the next up-and-coming engineer, right?"

"You know this, Mr. William," he joked.

"Well, are you going to dinner with Sam? That's his name, right?"

"Yes, knucklehead, and Sam loves the honeys just like you."

"What you mean just like me? And what about you?"

"I love the honeys too, but I'm not trying to give up the goodies so much, man. Too much to lose trying to get to my destiny."

"His destiny, meaning Elisa," Sam walked in, joking.

"Who's Elisa, big bro?

"Don't listen to him. She is just a lady that I once cared for years ago as a friend. But we knew how far to go."

"Yeah, she is all right. She was his student, and he let her get out of his life. And man, he be turning down the French honeys for a woman he only cared for."

"Come on, bro. Is Sam telling the truth? And if this is true, you need to handle up on that dame. How does she look? How old is she?

"Man, will you just change the subject? Sam is talking crazy as usual."

"She is beautiful, caramel, honey-glazed eyes, soft hair, and she graduated a doctor. And to top that off, she is intelligent, and her family is well-off."

"Hey, bro, where've you been hiding this lady, and does she have a sister?"

"No, she is the only girl, and her mother has three boys. And why am I telling you this? She is just a close friend that if it was meant, it probably could have been more, but since it didn't, I'm cool like that."

"I'm cool like that," Sam retorted after him, and Sam and his brother could not stop teasing him.

PAMELA GREEN

"Man, go get dressed and let's hit the town," Sam said.

As the boys went into the garage, they all paused as he pulled the cover off his Porsche. They stared at it like it was a Bentley or Rolls Royce or something. William walked over to it and kissed it on the roof.

"Hi, baby. Did he take care of my black beauty?"

"Man, now you're talking to a car. Yes, sir, you need a woman."

"I agree with Sam. You know he wouldn't let me drive that thing unless he's in it, but he let my dad drive it once or twice a month, just to wash it."

"That is crazy, man!" Crazy Sam teased.

As they got in the Porsche, he threw the keys to his little brother. He gave him that look like "I appreciate you." As they flew down the street in Pensacola, he started thinking of Elisa. He saw the exit to her home but didn't dare tell his brother to exit.

As they reached the restaurant, the ladies were standing outside waiting on Sam. As he got out of the Porsche, the ladies were smiling so hard. Sam walked up to them as if he was a king.

"How are you doing, ladies? These are my friends I was telling you about, my coworker William Harris and his brother."

"His brother has a name. Hi, ladies, my name is Lance, Lance a lot," he joked."

He was good to the eye just like William, and the ladies didn't know how to act with such handsome men. One looked at William, and she decided.

"Yes, this is the one I want," she told her friends, smiling.

William looked at her as if to say "I'm here for one woman and one woman only," but he didn't dare treat the ladies like how he was feeling. That's just the kind of man he was. He looked at his brother and Sam, and then he blushed. That one dimple showed, and all the ladies looked like they were about to melt.

"Hey, handsome, you are going to love this restaurant," one of the ladies flirting told William.

"I know, sweetheart. I'm from Pensacola. I've been here before. Let's all enjoy."

CAN'T STOP DESTINY

"Well, let's go in, shall we?" Sam said. "I haven't been here before, and I'm starving!" He reached his hand out, and one of the ladies grabbed it.

As the waitress showed them their seats, the men pulled the ladies' chairs up for them. As they sat down, they looked at each other. Lance noticed how beautiful the lady he was sitting by was. She was cute but very quiet. So that was kind of a turn off. But he thought to himself, *Her beauty made up for it.*

Sam looked at the lady he had on his arms. He thought to himself, *She will be one of my trophies tonight.* He smiled, and she smiled back, not knowing why he was smiling.

William looked at the lady that was interested in him. He said to himself, *She is not bad to look at, and she seems more intelligent than her friends.*

As they ordered, Sam and Lance broke the silence.

"So what will you ladies be drinking?" they said at the same time.

"I will have a skip, hop, go naked," the lady with Sam said.

"I will have a martini on the rocks please," Lance's date asked.

"I will have a diet Coke, thank you," William's date said. William was finding her more interesting after that. He was curious about the rest of the evening.

After dinner and good conversation, Sam had a plan. He just hoped William would go for it. "Hey, William, man, let me talk to you for a minute." He pulled him off from everyone. "Okay, now I know you are feeling your date, man. I saw how you both were at the bar alone, talking."

"Yes, man. She has a good head on her shoulder. I like smart women."

"Yah, yah, we know, but this is about tonight, man," Sam said sarcastically, knowing he was thinking about Elisa but didn't want him to break up the plan he had for tonight. So he hurried and changed the subject. "Well, it's like this. William, man, you have the crib, you have the car, and it's your call. The night is still young. We are on vacation. We don't have to work. So can we invite the ladies over, man, please?"

99

"Sam, I don't know, man. I'm not trying to have these women knowing where I live, thinking this is a regular thing." William took a deep breath, and he looked over at his date. She was really cool to talk to, and she has a head on her shoulder. It couldn't hurt. "Okay, Sam. Man, you and Lance better behave yourselves. Please, man, you know I know you." He smiled, hoping he wouldn't regret it.

"So," Sam said, walking back to his date, "would you girls like to come over for a nightcap?"

"Yes, we will love to bless the rest of the evening," Lance said, trying to sound sexy.

"Well, I don't know. We just met you guys. What do you think, ladies?" she asked her friends, hoping they would say yes.

"Well, if you follow us, we will direct you ladies to our castle," Sam joked but realized how William was looking and cut his joke fast.

As they drove up to William's driveway, the girls could not stop talking about how gorgeous his condo was.

"Okay, I know you ladies are not going to try, but I'm going to bless Sam tonight if he asks."

"You, slut. I told you she was going to give it up," Lance's date said.

"Listen, if he is packing like this, I know he's packing like this, if you get me!" she joked.

"Yes, we do, but William is really a nice guy," his date said. "I really want to get to know him better, if he'll let me. I can tell he is different from his buddies, and that is a turn on by itself."

As they walked in, William went to his CD and put on some soft R & B he had programmed to his music. As the stereo sound went all around the room, the ladies smiled at one another.

"This is really sounding smooth," one of the ladies said.

As they were pouring them and the ladies a drink, Maxwell came on, and Sam walked over to his date and asked her for a dance. Lance walked over to his date and asked her.

William walked over to his date, took her by the hands, and led her outside on his patio so he could get to know her a little better. As she walked out, she heard the ocean pounding against his fence. She could not believe the view she could see from his patio.

CAN'T STOP DESTINY

"This is nice, William. So are you guys renting this for the weekend?"

He blushed, with that one dimple winking at her. "No, this is actually my place."

"What! Come on, you're too young to be buying this kind of crib!"

"I know, right. You would be surprised what education and persistence will get you."

"So how old are you, if I can ask," she said, curious.

"I'm twenty-six. I'll be twenty-seven in two months, and I put down on this at the age of twenty-one. It was not as nice as it is now. I saved, put money into it. Six years later, this is what I have accomplished, with the Good Lord's help, of course."

"Yes, it had to be God. This is nice."

"Well, when I was teaching in Paris, I actually took advantage of the teacher's discount and lived in one of the student apartments half price, and I used all that extra money for the upkeep here and to pay the mortgage. I left my brother to watch it for me, Lance. And he paid me a little on it also. I had to teach him some responsibility, or what kind of big brother would I be?"

"So you and Lance are brothers. That makes sense now because he looks like you, just missing that gorgeous dimple." She smiled at him softly as if to let him know she was interested in getting to know him better.

"So you know a lot about me. So how long have you been living here in Pensacola, Florida?"

"I've been here about four years now. I'm from Orlando, but my job moved me here to help start up a team in the company I work for."

"So what do you do for a living?" William asked, liking what he heard already.

"I'm a doctor, and the company I work for has been in business now for about five years. They have a private family clinic. But it was started by a team of young doctors fresh out of college, and we are an amazing team. But my ex-boss told his nephew about me, and he gave me a chance to come help start and practice also in the business."

"So you are a doctor, so if I get sick, can you assist me for a discount please? You know what professors make," he joked.

They both started laughing, and they talked until four in the morning. As they walked in to get a nightcap, they noticed that the house was empty, but both cars were still outside.

"I guess your friends wanted a different nightcap," William joked.

"Yes, I guess so."

As the music was playing a soft melody, he pulled her close to him. As he looked at her with that dimple showing, she almost melted in his arms. He held her so close she almost felt like she was melting in his arms. As the music was about to end, he invited her up to his room just for relaxation.

"Okay, just for relaxation, right?"

"Yes." He smiled as he opened the door. She looked at the view.

"William, this is so nice. You are truly blessed, man."

"Thank you. Prayer and suffering got me this. When my friends were partying, I was making grades. When I graduated from college, I went straight to teaching at the high school right here in Pensacola. In fact, I was twenty-one, so the students thought I was their age."

"I know that was a little challenging because if you look like you do now, I know those young ladies were all over you. So did you behave, or did you fall for one of your students?"

William got quiet. He never forgot about Elisa. *But this woman made me almost come close*, he said in his head. Probably because she sounded a lot like her, and they were both smart and doctors.

"Well, I knew my boundaries, and I had a plan to fulfill. And I did that, and now that I'm a professor, I'm thinking about going back to school and open my own private school."

"Man, will you ever stop?"

"Not long as God keeps giving me breath." He blushed.

He grabbed her hands and pulled her down on his rug by his bed and held her in his arms. As the ocean was beating against the window, he looked her in the eyes.

"I really am enjoying your company, and I hope I blessed your night."

CAN'T STOP DESTINY

"William, you did."

He held her, and they both fell asleep in each other's arms.

As the sun was shining in the room, William jumped up and realized he was in Florida, and he relaxed and went to take a shower. As he was walking out, she was sitting on his leather sofa. She smiled at him as he walked out with a robe on.

"Good morning."

"Good morning, ma'am. If you want, I have some short sets a little too small you can put on, and you can shower before you go. I also have new toothbrushes in the medicine cabinet. Help yourself. I smell coffee downstairs. I must have at least one coffee before my day starts."

"Thanks, I will be okay. I will just use your toothbrush." She smiled.

As William walked down the stairs, Sam and Lance were blushing, and the ladies were staring at him too.

"So I see someone needed to sleep a little later than us."

"No, I didn't, sirs. I just took a shower, if that's okay with you two."

"Sure," Sam joked, "why not, sir. After all that, you need a shower?"

As William was about to answer Sam, the lady came down, and she had on his shorts.

"Okay, okay, big bro. So you are still alive, I see," Lance joked.

As William poured himself some coffee, he asked her, "Do you drink coffee?"

She said, "No, thank you. I will have tea if you have some."

William fixed her tea, and as they all were finished drinking, Sam asked if anyone was hungry.

"Well, you all are welcome to enjoy whatever is here. I haven't had a chance to go to the store. But I will pass. I told my parents I will be attending church with them."

"Church!" Sam joked. "Okay, now I've seen it all. You dance with the devil last night, and now you are going to church."

"Sam, man, let me school you. If I can dance with the devil all night with the breath God gave me, and if I could glorify the devil,

I'm definitely going to praise the one who gave me the strength to do it. Man, you are trying it, Sam. I put God first, and I always will. That's the way we were raised."

"Yes, we were," Lance said. "But I'm not going to church. I will be taking these ladies to breakfast because I haven't had a chance to make any grocery."

William's date walked up to him. "I appreciate you even the more. Men aren't made like you anymore."

"Yes, they are, baby. God proved that when you met me." He smiled.

"Well, here is my number, Mr. William Harris. Use it whenever you need a friend for anything. I mean anything."

She blushed as he took her hand and walked her to the car with her friends. As William was getting dressed for church, he blushed because he enjoyed a woman for the first time in a long time, and just maybe, he thought, *I can move on from my ghost, Elisa.*

CHAPTER 12

As Elisa was packing her last box, she was so happy to be moving back home. But she didn't know, she thought to herself, *Am I glad to be moving back because of my parents or Pensacola? I have an interview to do as soon as I get home, why not?* she joked in her head. Her friend Rhonda had asked her if she needed any more doctors to assist her with the other college students starting with her practice. And since the lady was already working in the field, she thought it would be an added strength to her team.

"Elisa, are you through yet? The moving company just called. They are close by," her mother, Autumn, yelled from the kitchen.

"Yes, ma'am, I'm on my last box," she said as she walked in the kitchen.

"I'm so happy my baby is moving home, and you moving in with us is even better, even if it's temporary."

"Well, I know the twins are driving Dad crazy now by themselves, so when I move in, I know they are going to drive me crazy too."

"I know, I know," her mother teased. "But it's just for two weeks. I am so proud of you and Stan Junior buying your homes so young. You'll be in there two weeks tops, so I will enjoy my baby girl until then."

"Thanks, Mom," Elisa said, putting her head on her mother's shoulders. "Mom, I'm almost close to my goals, starting my own practice at twenty and a half, which you know would have been hard if I hadn't saved almost all my savings from you and Dad and money from my jobs. Eating sandwiches and cheese crackers and fruit were worth it."

They both started laughing.

"Well, Elisa," her mother paused and looked into her eyes. "I hope a young man is in your plans. You are such a beautiful and wonderful woman. I know you have a vision, and you have always been driven for success. It's in your blood from your father and his father and even me with balance. Children make you stretch your vision, which I didn't mind. You all were worth it. But I notice that you don't go on dates. You don't talk about men much, except for one man that I could remember, and that was your teacher from high school whom you didn't even try to stay in touch with. I liked him. He was a little older, but older men are where it's at for a woman with a mind like yours."

"Mother, I understand how you feel, and believe me, I have seen a lot of men that I was interested in. But, Mom, they take too much of your time and energy. And as for William, Mom, I never told you this, but I really did care about him a lot. In fact, caring about him keeps me focused on what I need to accomplish."

"What do you mean, Elisa? He isn't your boyfriend, is he?"

"No, ma'am, but I had feelings for him that I or he couldn't explain, but our age difference and him being my teacher made us push what we were feeling back. But, Mom, I really did like him a lot. We spent the last two and half years together almost all the time. I helped in tutoring his students. I did his filing and his running for school supplies. We went to dinner and lunch together almost every other day. I would stay up late on the computer emailing him finished deadlines. It was bound to happen that we would start caring for each other, but him being my teacher, I cared enough to hold back my feelings openly and had them inwardly. He felt the same. He admitted it to me at my graduation party."

"Oh my god, all this time I have been telling you about his whereabouts, it's as if you were just admiring him for being a good teacher, and you are actually in love with the man."

CAN'T STOP DESTINY

"Mom, I did not say I was in love with the man. I said I cared a lot for him!"

"Young lady, you don't use a man that you just care about to hold you up and keep you strong enough to finish the things you have accomplished in four years, unless you are in love with him. And I bet you are still a virgin."

"Mommy!"

"What, Elisa? You know I'm telling the truth, and we are so close I'm surprised you kept this from me," her mother joked.

"Yes, I'm a virgin, and it's because I have two wonderful parents who raised me to fear God and wait for my husband. Not that I haven't been close before because wow, I have been close before."

"I bet it was Troy on your prom night because he's the only man besides William I had ever seen you have feelings for, I mean deeply. You were a mommy's baby all your life. You are even in the medical field like me because that was all you saw growing up. I just don't want you to miss out on the rest of growing up. A man doesn't complete you, but he helps you to complete, if you know what I mean."

"Yes, ma'am, I do, and I even thought about visiting Paris and seeing William when I go, just to see how his life has turned out. He used to email me every now and then, but then he stopped for some reason, and I stopped also. But one thing he did say before he stopped. He said that he will not have a part in confusing my goals and that I should focus on my studies and men will come and go."

"Oh, silly. He was not saying he didn't want you. He was saying 'I'm jealous, and I don't want you to mess with any of those college boys, just me,'" her mother joked.

Elisa got quiet, and she just stared out the window and pondered what her mother had just said. She thought, *What if that was what William meant, and if he did, why didn't he just tell me that?*

As the moving men came in to move her things to Pensacola, Elisa got into her faithful baby Cadillac her parents bought her for college. She said she would keep it until her business showed double profits. And it looked as good as when she first got it anyway. As she started the car, she sighed a sigh a relief but also a sad sigh. She was going to miss her place and the professors and friends she had made

107

at Florida State University. But they were only part of her plan, and she was ready to complete the rest of her plan. And she was wondering, *Is William going to be a part of it?*

CHAPTER 13

As William and Sam woke up, the rain was hitting on the top of William's beach home. The men were sitting in the kitchen, thinking of what to do on a rainy day, which isn't many in the summer in Pensacola. They looked at each other as William dipped bread into his coffee.

"William, man, where did you learn that?" Sam asked as he continually watched William dip his bread in the coffee he was drinking.

William blushed like a little boy, showing that one dimple.

"Sam, man, don't knock it until you try it. My grandfather taught me to do this when I was a little boy. I would sit with him on his porch, and he would dip his bread in his coffee and ask me to try it. I was only in elementary, but when I tried it, after the shock of the hot coffee, it actually tasted good, and I've been doing it ever since."

"William, let me try it because you've been doing this since I met you in Paris," Sam said, being curious.

After Sam put the bread in his hot Community coffee, he put it in his mouth. He frowned at first, then he said, "Humph! William, this is actually good, man. It's almost like milk and cookies."

Both men laughed so hard they woke up William's brother Lance. He walked in with no shirt on, boxers hanging to where you could see his six-pack and all.

"Man, won't you pull up your boxers!" William yelled. "We are not trying to get off on you, man. Dang."

"Hey, I can't help it if you old men aren't as sexy as me, and what are you laughing so loud for? I was trying to watch this movie on cable. You are interrupting my downtime. After a while, I'll be back at school and work. I need this rest. I don't want to look old before my time."

"Old," Sam joked. "Man, how old are you? Twenty-nine or what?"

"Man, William, tell your boy how old your little brother is," he said, pouring his coffee and showing his biceps. Lance grabbed some bread, looking like it was natural to dip bread in his coffee. Sam looked, shook his head, and smiled.

"Man, Lance, I guess you learned it from your grandfather too, right?" Sam asked.

"No, man. William taught me. I was not that close to my grandpa like William. I was a grandma baby. When I saw him doing it, I just looked, but he never told me why he did it, so I asked William why he did that. And he told me, 'You'll find out one day.' So when I got about in fifth grade, he told me to try it, and I liked it ever since. And it's a turn on to women. They love to see you look like a little boy, knowing you are a hard man."

"Man, you got jokes. You and Sam always find a way to put women in things—"

"Hey," Sam interrupted. "You know it's a man's world, but it wouldn't be nothing without a woman."

Then Lance and Sam started singing James Brown's song. William walked off as they were singing and went on his patio. As he sat down in the rocking chair on his covered patio, looking at the rain slowing down, he looked at the beach. It never failed to amaze him how he would see people jogging every time it rained. He promised himself he would try one day to jog when it was raining, but he never had. As he was sitting down, the phone rang. He just sat down, ignoring it, then Lance came on the patio handing the phone to him. He looked at Lance as if to say "I need some me time."

"Hello, this is William."

"Hello, sir. This is Thomas. How are you doing?"

"Thomas. Do I know you, sir?" William asked, curious.

"Yes, sir. I'm one of your students from high school."

CAN'T STOP DESTINY

"Thomas Edger! Man, what did I do to get this pleasure?"

"Well, sir, I just happened to be in Pensacola for this week, and I promised myself that I would keep up with the teacher that gave me the strength to go for my dreams. I called you every time I come home for the last three and a half years. But another man would answer the phone and tell me you were out of the country."

"Yes, that's my brother. He is living in my crib for me while he is in school. He didn't want to live on campus. And I am teaching in Paris now in a university, still a history teacher. I also work on the side for myself teaching computer majors how to build their own computers. I am so glad to hear from one of my students. So did you go to college as we planned and major in engineering?"

"Yes, sir. I do have one more year left. I thank you so much, and I'm on the dean's list. I mean the good dean's list."

They both laughed. William was so overwhelmed to hear from a student, especially those that the system thought would not make it.

"So what happened to your assistant, sir? I believe her name was Elisa Martin. Man, that girl there was so driven. And she was so driven guys were scared to ask her out. She would turn us all down in a heartbeat. I know she is making it big time, sir."

William paused. He was trying his best not to think of her but was yet hoping he would run into her. The last time he heard from her, it was by email, and he was feeling things he didn't want her to know, so he had sent her an email out of jealousy, asking her to focus on her studies, not men, that they would come and go. And she never replied, so he knew to just push off before someone got hurt.

"Sir, are you still there?" Thomas asked?

"Sorry, I'm here. I was thinking. Please call me William. I'm only six years older than all of you. William, man, please."

"Yes, sir, I mean William." They both laughed.

"Well, Thomas, I used to email her, checking on her. She should be graduating from Florida State University."

"Really, so what did she major in?"

"Psychology. Her mother is in the medical field. She wanted to follow after her. She is a social worker for the hospital here in Pensacola, but Elisa wanted to actually start a psych clinic."

111

"Man, that's impressive. I'm not surprised you know a lot about her. You guys were close. Mr. Harris, everybody used to tease you guys behind your back and say you were a couple. You were so close."

"No, man, no, they didn't!" William said, blushing through the phone. "Well, Thomas, the lady was very admirable, any young man will be blessed."

"Well, I haven't seen her since high school, but if I see her, I will be sure to tell her I talked to you. But, William, I'm doing good, and I'm moving back to Florida. I had a job offer from someone that knows my father, so I might finish my last year here in Florida. I just took a chance that you would be in the States. You really touched my life, and you gave me the drive to be who I am today. I wanted to say thank you."

"Thomas, you are so welcome, and that makes my teaching even the more worth it."

"So, William, when will you be returning to Paris?"

"Well, I should be returning on the first of August. I'll be teaching fall and spring classes. I took summer off to come check on my home and my car that I left here with my little brother and to see if I can see a few old friends, if you know what I mean."

"Yes, man, I do. I have a honey here, my high school sweetheart, in fact. But she and I commute back and forth for the last three and half years. I am actually engaged."

"Hey, congratulations. I really feel outdone now," William said, hoping one day he could be telling someone that. "Well, let me give you my cell number. Text me, and I will text you my out-of-state number and keep in touch with you, man. Have a good break."

"Yes, I will, Mr. Harris. I mean, William."

They both laughed and hung up. As he put the phone down on the table on the patio, he realized that it had stopped raining. The sun had dried up the water, and the beach was back in effect. As he could see the ocean waves coming on the beach, he thought of Elisa. *Man, I need to email her and see how she is doing after all this time. I really do care about her. She's a woman now, and hopefully, we can see what is meant for us once and for all.*

CHAPTER 14

As the twins were up early playing their Xbox 360, Elisa turned over and looked at her room which her mother had kept just as she left it. She looked at her end table and grabbed her class book. As she turned the pages, she noticed "Mr. William Harris." It was as if she couldn't breathe. She started blushing as if he walked into the room.

Okay, I have it bad, and I haven't talked to this man in years besides a few emails. What if my mother is right? No! I can't be in love with William. He was just a good and close teacher.

She smiled, grabbed her pillow, and screamed in it.

"I have to get in touch with this man, or I will never know our fate."

As Elisa was through dressing, she walked in the living area and tried to kiss the twins. Adam kissed her back, but Shawn said, "Hey, I'm not a baby!"

"You know what," Elisa said, hitting him on the side of the head, "you'll never get old as me, little boy. And just for that, I'm going to take Adam shopping this evening and not you."

"Hey, sis, I'm sorry. Here, kiss me, kiss me," Shawn screamed, trying to give Elisa his cheek.

"Are we going shopping for real, sis?" Adam asked.

"Yes, I have an interview to do, but right after it, I will take you guys shopping, and we can go eat pizza on the beach."

"Promise?" Shawn said excited.

"Really. In fact, you can go with me to my office and see it, and right afterward, we will go shopping, and to the beach we go. I want to enjoy you guys before you go back to school, and I get busy. If I wasn't starting my business, I would take you to Orlando to Disney World, but we got time for that."

They started to scream so loud their mother came out of the washroom looking like someone had gotten hurt.

"Boys, what, what…" she paused, looking stunned. "What is wrong?"

"Nothing, Momma," Elisa said as they ran off to get dressed. "I'm taking the boys with me to my interview, then I'm going to take them shopping, and we will eat pizza by the beach."

"Oh, thank you, Elisa. I need a break from the twins. They aren't bad, but they are a little handful. They love to eat all day, so when I'm home, I'm cooking all day. Or when they get out of school, they eat. After practices, they eat. I have to cook them healthy foods, or they will eat fast food every day, and since your dad is with them at practices, he feed them fast food all the time if I don't cook. So I work and cook, work and cook."

"Oh my god, Mommy, so this is what I have to look forward to when I have children. Bless you, but God blessed you with twins. At least Stan Junior and I were three years apart. I will be home now, so maybe I can help more with the twins, at least with downtime."

"How, missy? You are starting a business at the age of twenty-one, but I will assist if you have time to spend with your challenging brothers."

"Well, Mommy, I will try. I plan on being just like my mother one day. They will have to just live at the clinic with me like I did with you. And nowadays, we have computers, games, iPods, etc. to babysit for us."

They both laughed and hugged.

Elisa drove up to her clinic, and as she walked in, she was nervous. Knowing it's a Monday morning, she, with her assistants, would be practicing what they went to school for years to do. She walked into her office as the twins ran in other parts of the business

CAN'T STOP DESTINY

to see it. Elisa sat in her black leather chair which sat comfortably, and she looked up to heaven.

"God, I thank you for the wisdom to suffer and gain knowledge to get to this point." She had tears come into her eyes. She had all kinds of emotions—fear, joy, sadness of leaving Tallahassee—but "this was it," she said to God. "This is what it was all about, blessing your people you died for, helping me to be that Jesus they need in me."

As she wiped her eyes, the twins walked in.

"Sis, there is a cute lady here for you."

"Okay, boys, I need you to be my secretary and tell her to give me five minutes. Make her feel comfortable. Go over there in the refrigerator and offer her any drink she would prefer, okay, guys? And be big boys for me please?"

"I told you, sis," Shawn said. "We are not babies. We are big boys. You forgot we are eight, and we're about to be nine. We can handle this," Shawn said, smiling.

Adam was just blushing. He's the follower, even though he is the constructive one, Shawn is more outspoken. As the twins walked in to help the lady she was going to interview, Elisa walked into her office bathroom which she personally designed. It was a full bathroom with a shower in case she had long nights, with black marble finish and black dressers, drawers with gold glass handles. The floor was rock-built tile made of gold and black. She smiled as she made sure her attire was warm and welcoming for her maybe new employee.

"Hi, my name is Shawn, and this is Adam."

"Hi, young men. My name is Molina Dickerson," she said as she stared, seeing identical twins, making her blush. "I'm here to see Ms. Martin."

"We know. We are her brothers, and she will be out shortly," they both said at the same time.

"So would you like a drink?" Adam asked.

"Yes, thank you both so much. So what do you have?" she asked, smiling, noticing how handsome they were. She could not believe how they were identical but of different complexions. She thought to herself, *They are going be some knockouts when they grow up.*

115

PAMELA GREEN

"Ma'am, we have water, soda, cranberry drink, and some sparkling stuff," Shawn said, interrupting her thoughts.

"Well, I will have some cranberry. Thank you, young men."

"Would you like a glass with ice, ma'am?" Adam asked.

"Thank you. It will be much appreciated."

The boys went back to their sister's office and grabbed her drink. Shawn looked into the cabinet and saw some plastic wine cups.

"Man. Adam, she is going all out. Check out these glasses!"

"Look. Shawn, that is nice, right. And look how they look so real. I would have thought they were real glass."

"That's the point. Who's going to buy glasses over and over when these people accidentally drop one?"

"Hi, boys, did you help the lady? And did you get her name? I keep calling her lady. Let me look in her file."

"Her name is Molina," they said at the same time.

"Oh, okay. Good looking out, boys."

"Do you want us to bring her drink?" they said at the same time again.

"Okay, can you stop talking like one person?" she joked.

"Let Ms. Molina Dickerson in, and while we're having her interview, go in the waiting room, have a seat, and watch TV. It has cable too."

"All right!" they said, excited and were about to run out.

"Hey, you must walk and be professional. You are my secretaries today, remember?"

"Right," they both said.

"Hi again, Ms. Dickerson. Can we show you to her office?" Adam asked as Shawn took her hand, smiling.

"Yes, you may, sirs," Molina joked.

As Molina entered Elisa's office, she could not believe how elegant yet professional looking it was. She had heard how young she was and how intelligent she was at the same time, but she wasn't expecting this. Molina was twenty-five to Elisa's twenty and a half, and she could not believe someone so young could establish so much at such a young age.

"Have a seat," Elisa said as she turned her desk chair around. Elisa stood up and reached out for Molina's hand. "Have a seat please.

CAN'T STOP DESTINY

I have heard a lot about you from our mutual acquaintance, Rhonda, as I'm pretty sure she has told you. I have had this vision since my youth. Our goal here is to make a difference in the world of mental patients and their families. I'm looking for someone who is not in the business just for the money, even though we all need money. I need someone with a heart for my clients. I have a team of young doctors, as you might have heard, who have the same vision as I who will help me team it up. It will be called Family Business."

Elisa was smiling, but Molina could tell she was serious, and everything she heard about her was true. And she liked her style already.

"So, Molina, I also heard that you work for a family doctor practice, and you also helped them when they started."

"Yes, I did. At the time I was still in college, but I worked after my classes and on days I didn't have classes. Day and night at first when they first opened. At that time, I was young and driven just like you. I didn't start college until I was nineteen, but at that time, I was already a senior in college. I was twenty-two. I was excited to be a part of a family practice, and they are still going strong. But I like challenges and wanted to be a part of a small start-up business. I have to admit. The practice is not paying what I'm used to anymore because it started losing some of their clients to other practices that started opening up in the same building."

"Well, competition is going to be out there, and I will be standing on my God and the vision that he has given me and the many doors he has and will open for me to help us all be blessed as our customers will be blessed. So with that being said, I will show you a figure that we can afford for you in our budget. If you agree to the amount and the terms, we will need at least a year's contract signed. And it states that we can't lower your payment, only raise them, and you cannot leave unless under the terms stated on the contract. The team and I will love to have someone with your experience and drive to help us start out this practice. One question, have you ever worked with psychiatric patients? Because I see in your resume that you worked with families, but I don't see what kind of patients. We deal with people who have been abused, lost love ones, etc. We don't touch the bodies at all. We deal with the mind."

"Well, I will be honest. No, I haven't messed with psych patients. I mostly did physicals and pap smears and whatever the body needs. But I also dealt with low-income families that were very disturbed sometimes with prices and other issues that we had to handle one-on-one. I was patient and took care of their needs and complaints."

Elisa got quiet. She was thinking of questions that she didn't need any surprises later with.

"Well, Molina, not to be personal or in your business, but we are both young," Elisa joked. "And even though we are professionals, we also have our other side which needs some downtime. Do you have a family or any kids that will keep you from your duties? By this clinic just opening, it might take more of your time than your family needs."

"No, ma'am, I don't have any kids, and even though I met a man last night for the first time in a long time, I am not married."

"Well, I feel you with that, girl."

They both started to laugh.

"I don't know the last time I dated, and now that I'm so close to my vision being completed, maybe I will try to live a little. But first, I have to head this off and help us all get into place, and then I will take a much-needed vacation."

"I bet you do need one. Rhonda told me how driven you are. She really looks up to you."

"That's my girl and my only sister. Being the only girl my parents have and all, we've been close since forever. She is right. I am driven since my youth. Don't be like me. I had a chance for a great guy, and I let him go out of fear and what others might say. So how was the date last night, do tell?" Elisa joked

Molina joked back, "So does this mean I have the job?"

"Well, if you had a good date," Elisa joked back. "And you sound like a well-rounded person that this company can use. Don't get me wrong. I believe in family. I am so blessed, and my family was my strength. I have three brothers, one older than I, and those twins you saw took my place after fourteen years of being the baby."

Elisa held her right hand out, stood, and said, "You are welcome to this team. I'll see to it that your position after you give your two-

CAN'T STOP DESTINY

week notice will be waiting for you. But if there's any way possible, you can come part time in your two weeks when you're not working. We really could use the help. But you are not out about the date last night. Do tell!"

Molina was so happy to be a part of a beginning business. She also loved the figure placed in the contract that was put in front of her also. She didn't even care about last night.

"Well, Ms. Martin—"

"Oh no, let's get this straight. Now my name is Elisa, please. Yes, I desire respect as your team leader, but I can't do this without all of you."

"Okay, Elisa. I had a friend meet a guy that was visiting Pensacola for the summer, and she invited me and our other friends on a blind date with him and his friends. He is from South Texas, but he and his friend work out of the State in Paris, girl."

"Paris?" Elisa asked, being very curious. She hadn't dated in so long it sounded like something out of a movie.

"Yes, Paris, girl. And we all went out to dinner, and girl, when he showed up, we all were melting. I tell you, the man looks like something walking down from heaven."

"Really? Please do tell," Elisa said, still interested.

"Well, Elisa, when he blushed, the man had one dimple, and the way he smiled and his talk were so smooth. It was like the dimple was programmed to sink in his face as he talked. And to top that off, he is a professor in Paris. But girl, after dinner, he took us to his place. My friend's date was visiting with him. They both are professors in Paris."

"Man, me and Rhonda were thinking about going to Paris also. Maybe after all this gets rolling smoothly," Elisa said, still intrigued.

"Well, girl, he has a beach house that he bought when he was your age."

"Really, man. He sounds like he knows what he wants."

"Yes, he does, girl, and he lives, you know, where the beach kinds of curves. Well, his house is right there. The beach is at his back window, but the front of his house is like the corner of the beach, so he could sit on his porch and see people walking to the shore.

It's something out of a movie. And you know, that beach property is high-ticket now. Makes me a little jealous," Molina joked. "Well, to make a long story short, he and I talked all night till at least four o'clock and we…" Molina paused.

"What, girl, do tell," Elisa said, feeling alive for once.

"Well, well, we did not make love. We held each other all night. He got up, gave me some of his shorts and T-shirt to clean up in."

"And, and! What next, girl?" Elisa said, anxious.

"Elisa, he kissed me on the forehead, and he walked me to my car so he could go to church with his parents."

"What! Shut up. He did not. He sounds like an angel to me, Molina. Oh my god, where is a man like that for me?" Elisa joked.

"I know, right?" Molina laughed.

"So what is his name Molina. I know you got his name."

"Oh yes. Sounds just like some name out of a movie. His name is William Harrison."

Elisa paused. She felt like she was choking. She felt like her wind was taken out of her. She sat up in her chair. She smiled at Molina, a smile that's saying "please tell me you are lying."

"Elisa, are you all right, girl?" Molina said, looking at her worried.

"Oh yes. I'm okay. I swallowed my spit wrong," she said, barely knowing how to act.

"Well, Ms. Elisa, I mean Elisa, I will have some time to come by Monday and every day after that. I will let you know when I can come by and assist the team. I love your vision, and I'm glad to be a part of your team."

Molina held her hand out, and Elisa said, "So, Molina, what do you plan to do about Mr. Harrison? That's what you said his name was?"

"Girl, I don't know. He didn't leave his number, but I put my number on the side of his bed. Girl, I want that on my shelf, if you know what I mean."

Elisa halfway smiled. "Yep, I know what you mean. Let me walk you out, and I'll see you Monday."

CAN'T STOP DESTINY

As they were walking out, they noticed that the twins were deep into a Disney show on TV, so they walked by quietly.

"Elisa, you have some sharp little brothers, and the girls are going to go crazy looking at two look-alikes that are so handsome with different flavors they won't know how to choose," Molina joked.

"You are so right. I'm about to take them on the beach to eat. They have been so patient with you and I on a Saturday."

Molina put out her hand again, and Elisa said, "Girl, give me a hug. We will be partners Monday, which means you will be family."

So the ladies hugged, and as Molina drove off, Elisa grabbed her chest, and she could hear her heart pounding. As she walked into her office, she locked the door and fell to the floor, and she could not stop the tears.

She thought to herself, *How could I go on without William in my life? And to top it off, he will be dating my coworker?*

CHAPTER 15

As William was driving in the wind with the top down on his Porsche, he could not help thinking of the lady he met last week. He really liked her style, but he knew the only reason he liked her was because she reminded him of Elisa.

"Yes, Elisa," he said out loud to himself. "Will I ever see her again?"

He looked at the number Molina had left on the side of his bed on his end table. *Man, I might as well use it. Why not? Elisa is history. I need to let go*, he said to himself over and over as he drove.

As he reached his destination, he got out and looked at the campus that he taught at for so many years. As he walked to the front gate, he didn't expect anyone to be there.

"Hello, Mr. Harris. Long time no see," a man said to him. It was Mr. Jack, the music teacher.

"Man, what are you doing here on a Saturday evening?"

"I had a musical today with my summer school students, and we were just finishing on the last of the instruments that needed to be put up. So when did you get back into town, William? Last I heard, you were in Paris teaching."

"Yes, I am. I'm not teaching summer school, so I decided to come home for this month and relax for a minute. Two jobs can wear a man out, especially when you are speaking two languages all day."

CAN'T STOP DESTINY

"Man, you speak two languages all day. Bless you, and you already got the looks. I bet those French women be going crazy," Mr. Jack joked.

"Well, sir, I try to stay focused being a young professor as I am, have a little caution about the ladies."

"I feel you, man. We miss you around here. You were a good teacher and team player. Have you seen your little shadow?"

"Who, sir?" William said, sounding confused, not wanting to admit he knew who he was talking about.

"That young lady that always assisted you with your students. She graduated early. She was one of my best students too."

"Oh! Elisa Martin. Well, I know she went to Florida State University to be a psychologist."

"Yes, that's right. I also heard she has moved back. Man, you're not going to believe this. The young lady is starting her own psych family practice."

"Really, you don't say," William said, blushing for her. "So how'd you found this out, Mr. Jack?"

"Well, I saw her father one day. His sons play baseball with my son, and he told me she graduated at the top of her college class, and she saved enough to start her business."

"I just got back into town last week, Mr. Jack, so I haven't seen too many people yet. I was just passing by here reminiscing and saw you."

Mr. Jack started fondling over some paper in his tablet. He grabbed a pen, and he wrote an address down.

"Here, William, here is where the business is located. Go, see your shadow. I know she will be glad to see you. And I hope you have a safe trip back to Pareé," Mr. Jack joked.

Oh my god, William thought to himself. *What? Is this fate or what? Just when I was about to just go on and forget about the ghost of Elisa, I have her address to where she works. And she made it to her vision. I'm so proud of her.* He smiled so hard if someone walked by, they would have thought he was crazy.

"Okay, William." He started talking to himself. "You need to suck it up and go see Elisa. She is the love of your life whether you want to admit it or not. Okay, now you are talking to yourself about a woman that's supposed to be only a student. Yes! Right, you care more than you will admit. Wait, I said that already. Okay, okay," he said repeatedly. "I will just go over there next week. No, I can't do that. I feel like I'm stalking her! How can you be stalking a friend you haven't talked to in years?" He paused. He sat down on his hood, and he just smiled until he could smile no more.

As William drove up to his home, he noticed a car he did not know. So he parked into his garage and went into the house through the garage door. As he peeped around the hall door, it was Molina.

"Hello, Molina," William said, kind of happy but confused that she was there.

"Hi, William. I hadn't heard from you, so I wanted to stop by and give you my good news."

William thought to himself, *I didn't use your number because I didn't want to.* He remained quiet because he was a private person, and he didn't appreciate her forcing the issue. But he did like her, and he did think of calling her, at least that was before he found Elisa.

"Well, I see you have a drink already."

"Yes, Sam let me in. He went to use the bathroom, and we were hoping you would be here soon."

"Oh yes, I was driving around, enjoying Pensacola and missing my past students. I went by the high school. I even saw one of my coworkers. So what is your good news?"

"I got a job with this new family practice that will start next week," she said, excited.

"But I thought you liked the practice you were at already?"

"I do, but they had cut my salary due to fewer clients. With the new one, I will have a contract, and I can get higher pay, but it can't go down for at least a year. I like my boss already. She is so nice. But William, you are not going to believe this. The lady is younger than us."

William's eyes bucked, and he grabbed glass of cranberry juice and sat at the bar. He looked like he had swallowed an egg. Forget that, two eggs.

"William." She got up and walked over to him. She put her hands on his thigh. "Are you all right," she said, trying to show him she cared but knowing she wanted more.

CAN'T STOP DESTINY

"Yes, yes, I'm cool." He smiled halfway with that dimple showing. Molina took his hand and rubbed it.

"Hey," he said, moving her hand. Not wanting to seem rude, he apologized immediately. "I'm sorry, Molina. You caught me off guard."

"I'm sorry, William. I wasn't trying to impose. I really thought we clicked the last time we were together."

"We did, Molina. I don't mean to confuse anything, but I didn't want to call you unless I was ready to take it to another level. By the way, what is your boss's name?" he asked, dreading the answer.

"Her name is Elisa, and she is really cool. She has two handsome little brothers that were her secretaries," Molina joked.

"Her secretaries?" William said, confused, pouring vodka into his cranberry juice.

"Oh, while I was waiting on my interview, her brothers offered me a seat and drinks. They are so cute, if not handsome. They are identical twins. One has light-chocolate complexion, and one is chocolate, but that is the only way you can tell them apart. The young ladies are going to go crazy when they grow up."

"So this Elisa, how is she? I mean, did you both click?"

"Yes, we did. She seems like she is going to be a great boss. So, William, back to us. Can we go out for dinner, or would you like me to order in?"

"Well, Molina, I really can't do either. I had other plans. I'm sorry. I didn't know you were coming over."

"Oh, oh," she said, stunned. "I understand, William. You have my number." She walked toward the door. "Give me a call, William, and I hope soon."

She kissed him on the cheek. He opened her car door and told her goodbye with a half smile.

"Sam!" William screamed as he walked into the house.

"What's up, man. Where is Molina? Is she up in your room, man? You want me to leave so I won't hear you guys?"

"Man, get your mind out the gutter please. For once I have a huge problem!"

"What, man? What happened since I walked out this room and back in here?"

"Man, I know where Elisa is at!"

"Hush, man. That girl is in your room. That is rude!"

"Sam, Sam," William said hysterically. "She is not up there. I sent her home, man."

"Okay, you are scaring me, man!"

"Man," William said, sitting on the sofa, then lying down. He covered his head with a pillow. "Sam, this is not happening, man. This is not happening." He kept repeating.

"What happened? Man, you are scaring me for real. I never heard you raise your voice, man."

"Sam," William said real low, "Elisa is back in Pensacola. Not only is she back, man, she is Molina's boss."

"Shut up, man. Are you serious!"

"Yes, man. I'm so confused. Just when I was going to go on and let her go from my mind, she shows up. I went by the school this evening. One of my ex-coworker was there, and he told me she just started on her practice. I'm so proud of her. She wanted this all her life. That was all we talked about when we were alone."

Sam got quiet for the first time, and William put his head back under the pillow. Sam lay down on the floor and covered his head with his hands. As they lay down, Lance walked in.

"What's up with you, guys?"

Lance stopped and paused, looking at how weird they both were acting.

"Okay, either someone has died, or you two are going crazy."

"Man, Lance, I'm confused, and I don't know what to do," William said, with the pillow still on his head.

"Wait, wait! Who are you, and where is my brother, the one that is always humble, calm, and collective."

"Man," Sam, finally looking from under his hands, said, "Lance, your brother is in love with a woman he has loved since before he left Pensacola for Paris."

"What!"

CAN'T STOP DESTINY

"Yes, man, and the lady we introduced him to the other night just got a job with her."

"Oh, okay," Lance uttered. "This is some *Young and the Restless* stuff."

"Yes, it is because he was wondering if he should find her or not. And just when he was about to go on with his life, she shows up from every which way."

"William, is it Elisa?"

"Man, Lance, how'd you know?" William asked.

"Man, you were always with that girl. If you weren't with her, you were emailing her and texting her or calling her. You were just afraid because you didn't want to lose that job of yours, so you pushed her away. Man, we all knew you had it bad."

"Who is we?" William asked, sitting up now.

"Mom and Dad always asked me if I saw her. She was a freshman when I was senior, but when you were falling for her, I was in college then. But when I used your computer, I used to go through your emails," he joked.

"Lance, man, you are so nosy!" William said, pondering. "What were our parents doing thinking that?"

"Well, man, Mommy likes Elisa a lot. She would say, 'He keeps forgetting he is not that much older than that girl. They click well together.' Dad would say, 'So where is William Lover Boy?' He would joke behind your back."

William got quiet, and he realized that it all was true. But he didn't want to hurt Molina. *And how would that look, me going to Elisa to let her know how I feel and Molina being there on the job?* he thought to himself.

"Well, William, man, if I were you, I would make it known, man," Sam said. "William, we'll be going back to Paris sooner than you think. She has to know, or you are going to drive me crazy!"

They all busted into laughter and hit Sam with the pillows.

William walked off into his room, looking at the waves hitting against the back window. *Sam is right, but how can I make this happen without looking like a playboy?* As he was pondering this, he said to himself, *Elisa, I will make this right. I have to.*

CHAPTER 16

The practice was a month fresh, and they had many patients. The hospital where her mother worked had sent their extra patients to help with their overload. Elisa was taking the single patients, while her assistants took on the families. But whenever they couldn't handle the patients, they would give them to Elisa.

"Man, it's the end of the day!" one of the doctors said, sounding tired. "I'm out of here, Elisa. So what's on your agenda this evening? It's Friday, girl. Get out of here. Promise me, Elisa!"

"I have a few things to catch up on, and I'll be out of here, promise."

"Okay, boss, I'm holding you to it. I know you are the honcho, but we need you around here. You break, we're in trouble!" the doctor joked.

Elisa walked off and went to her secretary.

"Have you saved the first two clients to my database?"

"Yes, Ms. Martin, I have. It's ready for you to view over if you need to."

"Okay, have a long weekend. I have to go see how I can assist one of my patients, and then I'm off for the weekend."

"Yes, ma'am, I will, and you too. And don't stay late. It's Friday, Ms. Martin."

"Call me, Elisa, please. and thank you. I will see you Monday?"

CAN'T STOP DESTINY

Elisa walked into her office and sat back in her leather chair, breathing a sigh of relief. As she opened the file, she opened her mind to figure out how to help one of the patients find a living facility that is grant funded and which will escort her patient to sessions with her. That would be a relief for her mind, and she could assist her better. She started calling and made it happen. It took over an hour, but this was why she started this business.

As she looked over the second file, she saw what she was looking for. She smiled a sigh of relief, closed the Apple and went into her rest area, lay down, and fell asleep.

As the sun was rising in her office, Elisa realized that she fell asleep again in her office. Thank God that her security knew, when they saw her car, to set the alarm for her. Elisa got up and made her favorite coffee, Community. She walked outside and got a newspaper. As she sat in the break area, the phone rang.

"Hello, my friend, so what's on your agenda today? It's Saturday, and I want to go swimming. How about it?" Rhonda asked.

"Well, I took the boys to eat pizza a week ago. I promised myself I would go swimming before we get busy. Well, you know it's busy already, and I haven't gone swimming yet."

"Okay, it's a date then," Rhonda said, excited to be with her best friend.

As the girls reached the beach, the tides were high and white. They took their tent, cooler, and recliners and set them up. As they lay drinking their drinks, Rhonda looked at her friend who seemed very distant.

"Okay, okay, what is wrong with you? You are not yourself. This is the high point of your life. All our dreams for your business is coming to pass. Wake up!"

"Oh, Rhonda, I'm so confused and hurt at the same time," Elisa said while tears fell from her face. She tried to stop the tears, but it was years of tears stored up for the love of her life.

"Wait a minute. Why are you crying? Who hurt you, and why are you just telling me? You know I'm ready to break someone down for you!"

"I don't even know where to start, Rhonda. I just don't know what to do or how to handle this."

"Start from the beginning." Rhonda was now sitting in the middle of the recliner, anxious and angry.

"Well, you know how I feel about William—"

"William? This is about William?" Rhonda interrupted.

"Rhonda, please let me talk while I can."

"I'm sorry. It's just you have held back your life too long for a man you don't see anymore and who doesn't even know you care!"

"Well, he probably never will. He's dating one of my employees."

"What? Finish, Elisa, finish. I'm getting angry!"

"Well, I thought he was still in Paris, but he's here for summer break. And one of his friends introduced him to Molina, our Molina. She is a good worker, and our team is blessed to have her. She was sharing her date with me, not knowing the man she was talking about was William Harris. I have just been throwing myself into my work, trying not to deal with it and trying not to ask her how their relationship has grown."

"Oh, I'm so sorry, Elisa. How do you know it wasn't anything more than a one-time deal?"

"I don't, but I'm scared to ask."

"So you are going to let him go all the way to Paris and not pursue your feelings?"

"Looks like he has gone on with his life. What can I say? I don't need the disappointment."

"Okay, I won't push. I promise," Rhonda said, trying to wonder how to fix the problem already.

"He has a beach house over here somewhere. Molina already saw his condo. Sounds like a good investment too."

"Only you could think of business when you are hurting."

They both started laughing and ran into the ocean to swim. As they were getting out, Rhonda came up with a thought.

"Hey, let's drive down the beach. We have some time left before the sun goes completely down."

"I don't mind. There is nothing like a view of Pensacola beach when the sun is going down."

As they started driving, the beach was so beautiful Elisa felt like just parking and staring at the view from the pier. As they were driving, Rhonda was looking at the beach homes, trying to find William's home. As they were driving, she could not believe what or who she saw. It was William. He was checking his mail, with a white tee on and shorts, and he was as handsome as he was when he was their teacher.

If she wasn't my friend, Rhonda joked. *Now how can I get her to turn around so I can get that address? And if she sees him, she's going to think I set it up, and I did.* She laughed at herself.

"Hey, turn around. I want to go to that store. You are going too fast."

"What store," Elisa said, looking curious.

"Hello, are you going to turn around or what?"

Elisa turned around, and William had gone inside. She hurried up and wrote the address down.

"Hey, I don't see it. You are driving too fast, sis, just forget about it."

"You know what, you are tripping. I am going home. I need to rest!" They laughed as Elisa drove her home.

As Rhonda got in, she couldn't wait to find out if that was William. She took a shower and got dressed. "Why tarry?" she said. "We don't know when William will be leaving for Paris." She got into her car and drove right back to the beach. She laughed, turned her music up, and there she went.

As she parked in front of his home, she noticed someone sitting on the porch, but it wasn't William.

What if I have the wrong address? What if it wasn't him?" She just kept looking. She turned the music down, looked at the address again. As her head was down, someone knocked on the window. She jumped.

"Hello, ma'am, are you lost?" Sam asked.

Man, he is so handsome, she thought to herself. *I guess I better say something instead of staring.* "Hello, sir, um, I'm looking for my teacher. I heard he lives here. His name is William Harris."

"Oh, William, my boy. Yes, he lives here, ma'am. So what's your name, and how can we help you?" He flirted.

"Well, I don't know you to give you my name, but is Mr. Harris here?"

"Yes, he is. You can get out. I'll let him know he has a guest."

"Well, I don't mean any harm. I don't know you like that. You could be a murderer and could be the wrong address."

"Okay, stay here. I'll go get William for you, beautiful."

Rhonda smiled as he walked off.

Okay, now, Rhonda, what are you going to tell him if it's him? My friend is crazy about you. She's loved you all her life. Elisa will kill me if he didn't return the same feelings. Okay, here he comes. Play it cool, Rhonda. This is for your best friend.

"Rhonda Nickerson, hello!" He held his hand out to assist her out the car. She was a much-welcomed visitor. He felt like a spirit had gotten out of the car. Elisa's best friend, how can this be happening?

As she walked on the porch, she could not help but notice the beautiful ocean view, and the porch was so inviting. As he held the door open, she could not believe his home. It looked like a wife set it up, not a bachelor.

"Mr. Harris, this is gorgeous. Are you married, or have you been married?"

"No, not yet. I haven't been that blessed." He blushed. "Have a seat anywhere, Rhonda."

"Yes, anywhere," Sam joked. He was admiring her from afar, but she was too busy noticing William's house.

"So what brings you in the neighborhood, Ms. Nickerson?"

"Well, my friend and I were on the beach earlier, and I thought I saw you checking the mail. I didn't want to startle her. She was tired and trying to make it home. So I came to see if it was my favorite teacher. And here you are. I'm glad to see you, Mr. Harris. Your home is so—what's the word—handsome beautiful," she joked. "Well, if I can speak to you alone for just a moment, I would appreciate it." She looked at Sam, smiling as if to say "get out."

"Well, I see you guys need a moment, so I will return shortly."

Sam left, and as he was walking away, he looked back at her, blushing. She smiled back and sat back in her seat.

"Mr. Harris, do you remember our friend Elisa?"

CAN'T STOP DESTINY

He swallowed, knowing too well who her friend was. "Yes, I do. She was one of my strongest students and closest friend. She helped me out a lot with my students. But is she all right, Rhonda? Is that why you are here?"

"Yes, sir. She is doing okay. She just finished college in psychology. She also just started her very own family psych clinic, and she has a team of doctors that finished with her helping her."

"Man, she is everything I knew she would be."

"Well, Mr. Harris, she is almost complete. It's just one more thing she is lacking, and that's why I'm here."

As Rhonda began to talk and explain to him, the doorbell rang.

"I will be right back, Ms. Rhonda, and please, William. You are making me feel old, and I am only six years older than you, if not less."

"Okay, I will, sir. Habits are hard to break."

They both laughed as he walked and opened the door. It was Molina. She looked at Rhonda and Rhonda looked at William and she knew who she was.

"Well, come in, Molina. I was not expecting you this evening."

"I see," she said, looking puzzled at Rhonda. "So why are you here, Rhonda?" she asked as she hugged Rhonda.

Rhonda looked at William as if to ask "why is she here?"

"Hi, Molina. I'm an old friend of William, and how do you know Mr. Harris? William, you didn't tell me you had a date. I can return if you would like?"

"No, no. She is not a date. She is an associate, and we really need to finish our conversation, if it's okay with Molina?"

Molina pulled him by the arms and made him come down the hall to talk to her.

William looked at her, confused, and jerked away.

"Wait a minute. I really don't appreciate you handling me in front of my friend, and why are you here, Molina?"

"Well, I came to spend some time with you, but it seems like you have been too busy to spend some of your precious time with me!"

Rhonda was sitting on the sofa, and she could hear the entire argument. *She said to herself, I will not be leaving if that's what she thinks. Looks like a stalker to me!* Rhonda busted out laughing, trying not to be noticed.

"Molina, I apologize if I led you to believe we have more than what was planned. I really enjoyed your company, but my heart is with another, and the attraction to you was the fact…" He paused, not wanting to sound so forward. "The fact, is you remind me a lot of her, but you are not her, so I didn't want to lead you on. That is why I pushed away."

Molina leaned back on the hall wall. She could not believe what she was hearing.

"William," she whispered, not able to talk and embarrassed by what he was saying. "I really thought we clicked that night. And you did lead me to believe that you wanted more. Is it the lady in the front room, Rhonda?"

"Molina, again," he said, trying his best to be sympathetic. "It is not your business who she is. I really need you to leave, please!"

"William, how could you do this to us. We are so perfect for each other. How could you let another woman keep you from your destiny!"

"Destiny!" he screamed. "You are not my destiny. You are a woman I met on one date. I was cordial to you that night. That is who I am. I can't explain it any plainer, Molina!"

Sam came out of his room because he had never heard William get so upset with a woman before. *I do not want to miss the look on his face,* he said jokily to himself as he walked out the room, being nosy.

"Hey, you guys okay?" Sam said, trying not to smile.

"Sam, man, it's okay. I was just escorting Molina out of my home."

"You were what? I don't need your help. Mr. Harris, you will miss me!"

"Please! Molina, I really am sorry."

She looked at him and Sam. She burst into tears and ran out of his home.

Sam looked at William. He had never seen his friend look so helpless.

"William, man, it's not your fault you put that charm on her. You've been around me too long," he joked, hoping William would smile.

CAN'T STOP DESTINY

"Sam, this is not the time. I just hurt someone, and I didn't try to. I was just being me. That is why I don't like dating women. They take things too serious too fast."

William looked at him and then at Rhonda.

"Rhonda, I am so sorry you had to hear all of that. She was a blind date that reminded me of someone special, and I probably led her on, but I didn't try to, honestly."

"Man, Rhonda," Sam joked, "he has that Won Don effect on women even when he isn't trying, they fall all over him. And as usual, he is apologizing for being himself."

"William?" Rhonda said softly. She felt sorry for him, but after she talked to him and after hearing him, she knew she was right to come. She didn't tell him yet that she and Elisa knew Molina. "William, is the lady of your destiny Elisa?"

William could not hold it in any longer. He needed to be free. After five years of holding it in, he let it out.

"Yes, Rhonda, I'm in love with Elisa. I have always been in love with her since her senior year, but I was afraid of losing her friendship and the fact that I was her teacher. I didn't want to cross the boundaries. But, Rhonda, I have been in love with her since, and I've tried to go on with my life, but I can't stop loving her. And even living in another country did not change my feelings. I love Elisa Martin!"

The room got silent. Rhonda looked at Sam. Sam looked at Rhonda, and they both looked at William. William went to his dining area, sat at the table, and put his head down on it.

Sam and Rhonda walked over to him, feeling his pain, they said at the same time, "William, she loves you too."

"Hey, how do you know?" Rhonda asked, looking at Sam.

"Man, for you to come here and make up that lame excuse, she must be hurting as much as my buddy here."

William looked at Rhonda waiting for her answer.

"William, she does feel the same. She hasn't been with anyone since Troy, and she left him a long time ago. She has been working and going to school and planning her future since school. She is more driven now than she was in school. But she has everything she ever wanted, and reality is setting in. And she finally confessed to me that she loves you, but Molina works for her, and she is confused. She thinks you really care for Molina, and she is trying to cope with it. We were on the beach today, allowing her to vent her frustrations about the whole thing. And me, being the friend that I am—"

"We, we," Sam interrupted. "And I know you've come to fix it all, right?"

Rhonda looked at him and blushed.

"Yes, Sam. Yes, William. She's my best friend, and I love her like a sister. I could not let her go down without a fight and not knowing if it was all in her head about you, William. So now that you know, what now?"

William looked at them both and got up, and he hugged Rhonda so tight.

"You have to help me get her alone. I really love her, but she is working with Molina, and I don't want to hurt Molina any more than I already have. Besides, Molina is the reason I realize I had to face my feelings for Elisa. I didn't want to pursue Molina until I knew that Elisa didn't feel the same way. I just didn't know where Elisa was and how—I mean, when you drove up"—he was nervous—"to my door, it was God that sent you. Now I have to let Elisa know how I feel, but how?"

Chapter 17

As Elisa rolled over in her bed, trying to rest, she could not help thinking about all she had told her best friend. She had to admit to herself it was an overload release. But what she couldn't decide was if Rhonda was right by telling her to pursue her feelings. She didn't want to come into his life now that he had moved on with Molina. She liked Molina and valued her as one of the future top doctors if she stayed with the practice. She sat up and went into the kitchen. Her mother was still in the family room watching TV.

Elisa, go ask her, she said to herself, staring at her mother as she poured herself some cranberry drink. She tried not to disturb her mother by gently pushing the crushed ice button on the refrigerator.

Her mother turned and spoke, "Hi, my love. What are you doing up? I figure you would be resting after the long day you had."

"Yes, ma'am. I just needed a drink. So what are you doing up, ma'am"?

"Your dad is watching something I didn't want to see, and it's a good movie on that I wanted to see. I'm through crying. It was so good. It's off now. You okay, right?"

This was her chance. Speak now or forever hold her peace. "Yes, ma'am, well…"

"Is that a yes or a no, young lady?"

"Well, Mom, it's something I need to get off my chest, if you have time."

PAMELA GREEN

"Well, it's only twelve midnight," her mother joked.

"Mommy, I've come to a point in my life where I really don't have plans, and I'm trying to go forward, but I don't want to make the wrong moves. You know what I mean, right? You've been here, I know."

"Hey, are you calling me old?"

"No, Mommy, but you are my mother. Who else would know the answers besides Grandma?"

"I will ignore that statement, young lady. Now what is your question?"

"Well, Mommy, you know I have a vision for my life, but there is something you don't know. Only Stan Junior and Rhonda know."

"Okay, if your brother knows, and he didn't help you, it must be big."

"Well, Mom, it's like this. I'm in love with a man."

"What! A man, and I didn't know? I'm hurt!"

"Wait, Mom, don't get upset. You know the man."

"I do? And how do I know him when I never see you with anyone besides a computer and a notepad? Out with it. Who is he?"

Elisa paused. She feared her reaction. "Mom, it's William Harris."

Her mother smiled, got off the studio chair, and sat next to her daughter on the sofa. She looked her in the eyes. As she looked at Elisa, Elisa stared back and got teary eyes.

"Don't cry, honey. Your father and I always knew you and William cared about each other. That is why we invited him to your graduation dinner. We thought since you had graduated, and you were so mature and smart for your age, we could understand how you would fall for an older man. And besides, he is not that much older than you. But when you never react when I bring his name up, I thought you had lost interest."

"Mom, you knew all this time, and you didn't tell me? Oh, Mom, I'm so confused." She busted out laughing out of relief and joy. "Well, what should I do? He is in town, but he is dating—you are not going to believe this—one of my employees."

"What! Oh my god, Elisa, how did you find this out? Is it our William?"

138

CAN'T STOP DESTINY

"Yes, ma'am. Fate set it up. That is all I can say. She was telling me about this incredible man that just happens to be my William."

"Okay, Elisa. So does William know how you feel?"

"No, I only told Rhonda today how I feel and how I have come to a crossroad in my life, and it ended up with William not in it. You know he was my strength that helped me to reach this point in my life. I mean, Mom, I…" She paused for a moment. "I was hoping fate would put us back into each other's life. And it helped me to suffer and focus on my vision for my life. But now that I have what I always desired for, I don't have him. And I really like Molina. She is a good asset to the company. She reminds me so much of myself."

"Well, Elisa, if she is dating William, I'm sure it's because he sees a lot of you in her. I don't mean to sound like the psychologist." They both laughed. "But God has given us one life and he gave us choices and he gave us a will, desire, and emotions to top them off with. You won't know the will of God for you and Will's life until you confront him. Molina, that's her name?"

"Yes, ma'am."

"If you care about her like you say, she deserves for you to confront your feelings once and for, all young lady. I mean, that's my diagnosis, doctor."

"Mommy." She hugged her tight and smiled, then stared off.

"Hello, are you still here?" her mother asked as Elisa looked off into space.

"Um, yes, yes, Mother. I just got nervous. This is not just another man. This is William Harris. I've loved this man since he walked into my life five and a half years ago. How will I make this happen, how?"

"I don't know, young lady. But you need to do something before Molina runs off with your husband. You better not give that away, young lady!" her mother yelled, making her jump.

"Okay, okay. Let me pray about it and see how God and I can make this happen."

"There you go. That's the woman I raised."

Meanwhile, as Rhonda, Sam, and William were sitting at the bar in William's home, they could not come up with anything yet. They just drank coffee and listened to Najee. Sam finally said something.

"Okay, we know you can't go to Elisa's job. Molina will go off on the both of you as if you set it up to be together."

"Right," Rhonda said, looking at her clock. "Man, it's that late, William?"

"Yes, it is, Rhonda. You can sleep in my room if you want, and I'll sleep on the sofa. I feel safer than you driving home at two in the morning."

"Thanks, William. That's why you were my favorite teacher. You always put us first."

"That's why I teach. I really care about my students as well as others. Which brings me back to Molina!"

"Yes," Sam said, sounding sleepy. "So we are all mature adults who can't come up with a plan?"

"I got it," Rhonda said, almost falling out of her seat. "Well, Elisa keeps saying she needs a much-needed vacation, and she was talking about taking me to Paris. I wonder why!"

They all looked at each other and laughed so hard they couldn't sit in their seats.

"Well, we know why now," Sam said, joking. "She was trying to sneak in on the love of her life, Mr. William Harris."

"Sam, man, you are on a trip, but I hope you're right this time," William said as he walked to the window, looking outside, admiring the moon on the beach. "Man, I love her so much. Sam—"

"Well, like I was saying," Rhonda interrupted them. "Hello, I was trying to give my opinion. Well, I can talk her into going on that trip that I really need. And, William, you can go back, and we all can hook up in Paris!"

"Hey, that just might work. We can cut our trip short," Sam said. "Then we can make it happen for you guys. I'm going to miss the beach, but I need to go back and take care of few things before classes start anyway."

William paused and opened the door. He sat on the porch, listening to the waves. As he was sitting there, his brother drove up.

"So what wind blew you in this time of night, man?" William asked.

CAN'T STOP DESTINY

"Man, I was doing me, you know, big bro. I was with one of the honeys. So why are you still up?" he asked as he stared in the house, seeing Rhonda in the refrigerator. "And who is that? I see you've been busy too, man!"

"Stop assuming, man. Everybody doesn't need their rocks to be released like you, little bro. Well, if you might know, that is one of my students, and she came to visit."

"Until two in the morning. You have been visiting all right."

"It's a long story, but I have some good news."

"What? You are going to give me your car?"

"No, for the final time."

"I might be leaving for Paris sooner than planned, and you can have your bachelor pad back."

"Yes! Because I've been spending money that I can be saving, but you and Sam are cock blocking."

"You know, you need to slow down, man. Women aren't going nowhere. And besides, I'm trying to be with the one, man. Too much time on your hand, little brother. I can always get a woman. I want my woman. You feel me!"

"Whoa, who is the one? And when did you ever find her? Every time I try to hook you up, you're just blowing the chicks off. I have to meet this one for sure, especially if she has my brother's nose open."

"Man, little bro, this nose has been open for five and a half years. I'm just tired of worrying about people."

"Okay, who is she? What's her name, Will?"

William sighed, blushed, got up, and walked to the end of the porch.

"Her name is Elisa Martin."

"Elisa! Your student, the one that was always at the house working with you before you moved out? Man, she was a hoity!"

"Hey, man, you are talking about the love of my life, my future, I hope."

"William, she was nice, and you wouldn't let me hit on her. Now I know why. You have good taste, bro. I would have waited for that one too."

141

William smiled a sigh of relief. "Yep, man, she is the one. She is the reason I was so strong over these years. I was waiting and hoping fate would put us back together, but as always, I let people and what they might think keep me from pursuing her."

"Well, I saw what you emailed her before."

"Hey, how'd you know that?"

"Well, when you visited last time, I saw your email to her. You had left it open. But you told her you were not going to have a part in confusing her and that she should focus on her goals."

"What? I said that? Are you sure?"

"Yeah, man, I read it and said to myself, *He is still being a teacher.* I thought then you should have made something happen, but you pushed her away."

"Man, maybe that is why she stopped emailing me. Oh no, I led her away all by myself!"

"Yes, you did, bro. I thought that was what you wanted, so I just stayed out of it."

"You picked the wrong time not to nag, little bro."

William walked back into the house. Sam and Rhonda were sitting on the sofa. She had fallen asleep, and he fell asleep next to her.

"Rhonda, let me help you into the bedroom," William said, smiling. He felt like he owed her his life. She was making the one thing in life that will complete him happen.

CHAPTER 18

Elisa woke up early. She went into the office to make sure her plans to go out of the country didn't interfere with the practice. She had so many plans for this week. She started feeling overwhelmed. But she knew that she needed a vacation, very much, after finals and going straight to work day and night. She thought to herself, *Maybe I'll just find a way to call him or email him.* No, that will be so impersonal, and William meant too much for her to just call or email. She picked up her phone, sat in her office chair, put the phone on mute so no one could interfere with her phone call.

"Hi, Rhonda, where are you? We need to talk?" she said.

"Hi, Elisa," Rhonda replied. Looking around in a room with the sunrise coming from the beach. She felt like she was in another time or place. As she sat up in the bed, William knocked on the door.

"Elisa, let me call you right back. Someone's calling in, and it looks important."

"Call me right back, promise. This is very important, please!"

"Come in," Rhonda said, feeling like a princess in this gorgeous room. *This man had to have been married before*, she thought as she looked around.

"Hi, Rhonda. Hope you slept okay. It's early, but I didn't know if you had a job or not, and I didn't want you to miss out on your denarii," William joked.

"No, I'm actually off today. I choose to be off on Mondays and Sundays so I won't be worn out for partying and work the next day. So how can I help you, William?"

"Well, I brought you some fresh towels, and I brought you a new toothbrush."

"Okay, now you had me at the furniture. What man has new toothbrushes unless he has a wife or…" She paused.

"Or what?" William asked. "Hey, I'm not gay, if that is what you are asking."

"Well, man, your house is too fly for a bachelor, and you have taste like a woman."

"Well, maybe that is because for one, my mother and father had taste. I've been living by myself for years. And I always stayed close to my grandmother who also was a teacher. And being single all my life, so it was just put in me. But believe me, I am into the ladies. There's just one lady that I desire now, and you know who that is."

"Okay, I can relate to that. I was raised by my grandparents too, but for style, my grandparents did not have too much. But they were clean freaks."

They both laughed, and then they stared at each other.

"Okay, William, if you must know, that was Elisa on my phone. She asked me to call back and that it was important."

William felt nervous. "Well, it's your time to make it happen, Rhonda, please!"

"Okay, I'll call her back."

"Thanks. When you finish, I've made some coffee, and if you want, you can come in and help yourself to some breakfast.

"Thanks, Mr. Harris."

"Rhonda, after all we've been through in the last hours, Mr. Harris? Come on, lady."

Rhonda blushed.

"Okay. Well, let me call our girl."

As Rhonda picked up the phone, she was as nervous as William. "What am I going to say to convince her to go to Paris? Money, time, last minute—she is going say no. I just know it."

CAN'T STOP DESTINY

As the phone began to ring, Rhonda was pondering what she would say to ask a question about a trip she barely could afford, but she knew Elisa could, so she bit her bottom lip and let her have it.

"Hi, I'm calling back. So what is your important news? I hope you are all right?"

"Yes, I am, but I had to get your advice before I change my mind or someone else would walk in my office with a file that will make me change my mind."

"Okay, now you are worrying me. What is it? Speak, please."

"Well, do you remember I asked you if you would like to go to Paris so I can get some downtime?"

Rhonda paused before answering. *She could not be making it this easy for me*, she joked in her head.

"Yes, Elisa, I remember."

"Well, since I've talked to you, I've talked to Mom, and she has convinced me to go and look for William."

"Shut up. She did not!"

"Yes, she did, and I am going to do it, but I can't do this alone. I need my best friend with me. Please!"

"Girl, you had me at Paris, but how soon? And do you know how much money that is going to cost us, especially at this last minute? The flight tickets are high with last-minute reservations, and you know you and your family only ride first class. Hello, I'm blessed, but my money doesn't roll like that, sis."

"Don't worry. My father has connections with the airline. My mother has connections with hotels in Paris because of her frat sister. And you know I've been stashing for my dream vacation. See, being uptight and to myself missing William paid off." She laughed. "And now I can afford to go see the love of my life."

Silence came over the phone as Rhonda was still laughing, excited about the trip of a lifetime.

"Hey, are you still there?"

"Yes."

"I know your office doesn't have drop calls, why the silence?"

PAMELA GREEN

"Rhonda, what if he has someone in Paris? And what about Molina? I know he is in town, but I just don't want to throw myself at him. Even though it would save me a lot of money if I did."

"There you go, second thinking and worrying about everybody else's happiness except for Elisa Martin."

"You're right. See, that is why I need you with me. And besides, I need to catch up with my body. After dealing with finals, graduation, starting this business, and dealing with so many hurting people, I didn't realize how much energy it takes. I'm also dealing with my realtor, hoping we can meet at the table tonight to close on the house. So this is something I need so I can focus on the problems at hand, my business and my man."

"Yes, that's what I'm talking about!" Rhonda yelled over the phone, making William knock on the door. "Hold on, Elisa."

Rhonda put the phone down, walked to the door, and whispered, "Hey, I'm on the phone with Elisa. Good news."

"I was worrying. I heard you screaming."

"Oh, I'm all right. She was just giving me some good news. Give me a few more minutes."

"Okay," he said, looking nervous.

"Okay, Elisa, what is the plan? Let's make this happen. Give me dates and time. Let me know what you need me to do."

"First, how much money do you have for the trip? I will email you Ms. Tramper's number and just let her know that we will need a flight to Paris Wednesday as early as possible."

"Wednesday? Aren't you moving a little too fast? We have to do our nails, hair, feet, and I need to buy me some luggage."

"Do you want to go or not?" Elisa said, sounding serious and businesslike, which always made Rhonda stand to attention.

"Yes, I'll be ready. I have to take some of my personal time as this is important. That was good thinking on the company's part. They knew they would have a Rhonda in their company that would have to leave out of the country suddenly."

"Yes, and I'm my own boss, and I have a strong team. Besides, my mother said she would come and run it for me until I come back. You can't trust anybody but God. You know my saying, love every-

146

CAN'T STOP DESTINY

body but trust nobody. Hey, we are all human, and it leaves room for forgiveness when you or someone else is not acting perfect as we are supposed to be in Christ Jesus."

"Okay, now you are preaching to me. Where is this coming from?"

"Rhonda, you know I was raised to know better, and besides, God has been my strength and hope for years. I'm just recognizing this is fate, and I'm going to give it to him!"

"Amen to that, sister. Well, let's go get your man! Email me, and I will make it happen."

"I love you, Rhonda. Thank you. Let me go. My phone is ringing like crazy. And I will pay for whatever you can't afford this time."

"Really? Thanks, sis. I love you too."

As Elisa hung up, Molina knocked on the door.

"Hi," she said in a sour voice.

Elisa looked at her, sat up in her chair, and sighed in relief, but she didn't know how to act. She knew how Molina felt about William. She felt terrible, but she loved him first, and she had to know.

"Hi, Molina, please have a seat. Can I get you a drink?"

"No, Elisa, thank you. I just need some of your downtime."

"Talk to me. I have a few, but just a few."

"Well, it's really nothing that I didn't bring on myself. I caught William with another woman last night."

"What!" Elisa sat up. She felt like she had swallowed a frog. Her heart felt like it was stopping up. "What do you mean you caught him with another woman?"

"Well, it wasn't really that he was with her, but it's what he said to me while she was there."

Someone knocked at the door.

"Hold on, Molina. I will let them know we are in conference."

"Hi, Elisa. Your first client is here."

"Can you make sure they are comfortable? I'm in a small conference and do not want to be disturbed. By no one, please."

"Yes, ma'am. I can take care of them."

As she sat back down, she could see the hurt in Molina's eyes. She felt the hurt, and she was hurting as well.

"Elisa, he was acting as if he didn't know me, and he actually raised his voice at me. And that is a side of William I have never seen. He asked me to leave as she stayed there, and this is what hurt me the most. He told me that he was in love with someone else and that the only reason he dated me is because I reminded him of her, and then he started showing me the side that made me start to, start to…" She paused and said before crying, "He made me start to love him!"

"You love him, Molina? How? You told me you two barely dated!"

"Elisa, he is not like other men. I never met a kinder, sensitive, and well-balanced and controlled man in my life."

"Well, he wasn't that last night from what you are telling me," Elisa said, feeling angry inside.

"That's just it, Elisa. Even though he hurt my feelings, he still was trying to protect them. I just fell all over him in front of her and his friend."

"Who was she then if she wasn't the one he was in love with?"

"Her best friend. She was obviously over there helping him to keep or get her. I don't know," she said, sobbing harder. "I just know I love him, and I wanted to be the one!"

Molina was so upset she forgot to tell her it was Rhonda, their mutual friend, who was over at his home. Elisa forgot he was the man that she loved and got up as the doctor she was and held her tightly.

"Molina, you are stronger, and you will overtake this problem. It was better that you found out now before you fell in love with William."

"I know you are right, Elisa. I just needed to get it out before it overtakes me. I drove by his house early this morning. I even called his house leaving messages about how I thought he was the one for me. I feel so weak but, girl, love makes you do that!"

Elisa just held her, paused in her heart, and before she knew it, she was dropping tears that could not stop.

"Molina, I'm so sorry for crying. I just know how it feels to love someone so badly that you can't breathe without him. I tell you what. Take off today with pay, but the assignment for you is to go home and write down "why I love myself outside of a man." And after you

CAN'T STOP DESTINY

realize how much you love yourself, forgive William. Remember we are all trying to get to where he is at, and you can't make your heart do what your mind wants it to. And he obviously loves her if he told you in such a desperate way. And you said he even tried to protect you after he hurt you. I see why you love him. I would love him too."

Molina hugged her so tightly.

"Thanks, boss. That is why I transferred here. You have such a big heart. Your customers and future hubby is going to be so blessed."

They both laughed and hugged as Elisa wiped Molina eyes and her own eyes as well. As Molina walked out, Elisa went into her private room in the back. She cried so hard, and she called Rhonda.

"Hello, Rhonda."

"Elisa, is this you? What is wrong? I just talked to you, and you are scaring me."

"Rhonda, you will not believe what Molina just told me. I am cancelling our trip as soon as possible now!"

"Wait, wait," Rhonda said, panicking herself. This was a trip of a lifetime, and she hadn't even had time to tell William how Elisa was going to meet him. "Okay, what did she say? Please calm down and talk to me. In fact, I'm on my way!"

"No, Rhonda, do not come. I will be all right. I have clients waiting on me, and I just need you to postpone the plane tickets. Tell me you haven't made reservations yet, please!"

Rhonda paused, and she lied. "Yes, I have, and that is a lot of money to lose. We have to talk. I'm on my way."

Elisa went into her bathroom, washed her face, and put her makeup back on. As she walked back into the office, she felt numb and more driven than ever. She already was planning to drown herself into her work. As she sat at her desk, she swallowed some of her cranberry drink and called her secretary in.

"Tricia, you can bring the client in now. Did you take care of them for me? Don't answer that, Tricia." She smiled. "I know you did. Thank you. Send them in please."

CHAPTER 19

As Rhonda was driving, she was dialing William's number. She was moving fast and thinking fast. She had to make this happen one way or another.

"Hello, Rhonda. Is everything okay?"

"Hey, how'd you know it was me? Forget the question. Don't answer it. We need to talk yesterday!"

"What's wrong," he said, not wanting to panic, hoping nothing was wrong with Elisa.

"Molina talked to Elisa, and she is so upset. She was about to go to Paris, but whatever Molina told her made her postpone the trip!"

There was silence on the phone as William collected his thoughts. He realized that he must go over and face Elisa once and for all.

"Rhonda, I am going over to her office. Forget about the trip. I will not lose her. I love her, and I'm on my way."

"Okay, but, man, Will, I'm going miss my trip to Paris."

"You still might end up going if I have my way."

"So you really are going over there?"

Rhonda realized that the moment her friend had been waiting for all her life was about to happen.

"Hey, William, let me go too. I want to be there just in case it doesn't go down like you are hoping."

"I don't care who is there—you, Molina—but I'm on my way now!"

150

CAN'T STOP DESTINY

As William drove up and parked, he felt butterflies that he hadn't felt since he first saw her, and she was in high school. He wanted to imagine the worst, then the best, but he was determined to go in that building and get his future wife.

As he walked in, he could not believe how immaculate the building was. It was so unique, and the atmosphere was so perfect. He was sure the patients never wanted to leave as he saw children playing while their parents were reading. Some were drinking, others watching TV. He just could not believe how special this lady really was.

As he stood at the front desk, he exhaled and said it, "Good evening, may I see Ms. Martin please?"

"Do you have an appointment, sir? She is well booked today if you don't have."

"Ma'am, this is important, and she will want to see me."

"Let me ask her, and can I have your name, sir?"

"Yes, ma'am. Tricia, is it?"

"Yes," she said, about to melt because as he said her name, she was melting as he was speaking. She was hoping he wasn't crazy and was available.

"How do you know my name?" She blushed.

"It's on your desk, Ms. Tricia," he said softly as he blushed, and his one dimple showed.

"Um, sir, let me call her. Have a seat please, and you are welcome to take this ticket and get a drink. It's complimentary of Ms. Martin."

As he walked and got a drink and sat down, Tricia forgot to call for looking.

"Ms. Martin, um there is, um..." Tricia could hardly speak.

"Tricia, are you all right? And stop calling me miss, please."

"Sorry, Elisa."

"Thank you. That is more like it. So is my next client in? I should be having one more before I call it a day."

"No, ma'am, but there is a gorgeous man out there that said he needs to see you, and it is very important."

"Really? Is he a psych patient?"

151

"No, ma'am, he's far from being a psych patient, and if he isn't your man, can you introduce him to me please? He isn't crazy, but he is driving all the ladies in there crazy!"

They both laughed and walked to the door.

"Well, show me this god."

"There he is, the one drinking and talking to those children."

Elisa's mouth flew open. She could not believe who it was. *I must be dreaming*, she said in her head. As she stood there mouth wide open, she just stared at him.

"Um, Ms. Martin, this is Mr. Oh, sir, hello. I did not get your name."

William stared at Elisa, and he did not say a word.

They both stared for at least ten seconds before Tricia said, "Okay I gather you know each other, and you are not my kid's father." She was joking, trying to change the awkwardness.

They continued to look at one another. Elisa turned around and walked to her office. William looked at Tricia as if to say it's okay. He walked in after her and closed the door.

"Elisa, please say something. I will not leave like this. I need to know that you love me like I love you."

Elisa turned around in her chair, faced him, and said, "How dare you walk in here talking about love? I've waited over six years to hear you say that, and after all you are doing, you come and say it now? Why William, or is it Mr. Harris?"

"Elisa, you are confusing me, and it is William, Mr. Harris, whatever you need me to be, lady. I love you, and that I do know. And I don't care if Molina knows it, the school district, anyone. I can't breathe without you anymore!"

"So you are the Mr. William that Molina is in love with. You broke her heart for someone else, and if you are in love with someone else, William, why are you here?"

She was screaming so loud. Her coworkers had never heard her raise her voice. They all rushed to the door out of concern.

"Ms. Martin, are you all right?" they said on the other side of the door.

CAN'T STOP DESTINY

She burst into tears, and William ran up to her and held her so tight she could hardly breathe.

"I'm, I'm all right," she said on her mike on her phone. "I'd be out shortly. Can you ask Karen to take my last patient please, Tricia?"

"Yes, ma'am."

As she took her phone off the receiver, she realized that she was in William's arms, and it felt right. It felt like home. And she thought of what Molina said, and she began to cry again.

"Why are you crying, baby? Don't you know it is you that Molina is talking about?"

Elisa pushed back and looked up into his eyes. His eyes were full of tears. He moved down and kissed her like his life depended on it.

As he pulled away, he took her chin in his hand and said, "Elisa Martin, I've loved you since I first saw you. I was so afraid of what I was feeling I just kept you close as a good student. Every time we were alone, it took only God to keep me from it. I prayed a lot over the years, and when you stopped emailing me, my world stopped. I tried to date other ladies, but they just couldn't give me what I needed, and that was you. On your graduation night, I was about to tell you then, but I thought of your age and your future, and I loved you enough to let you go."

Elisa smiled inside. She could not believe he felt the same as her. She put her arms around his waist softly and pulled him to her closer as she looked into his eyes and watched how he blushed with his one dimple from her advances. She could feel him shaking, or was it her?

"William, I loved you ever since you walked into our classroom to be our teacher. I allowed you to keep me close because I was so afraid if I made any advances toward you, I would get expelled. I had a goal to reach, and being expelled was not a part of the plan. I could tell you were attracted to me, but since you never proved it, I was afraid to make any advances. That night on my graduation, I wanted to tell you also how much I love you. But with the fear that I was too young, and you were so mature and handsome, I knew you could have any woman you wanted, so I just pulled back.

She hugged him closer as the tears started to roll down her cheeks.

"William, you were my inspiration. You gave me the drive I needed to finish college and not get caught up in the men that were making advances toward me. The night I decided that I would break out from being a virgin—"

William's smile turned into a frown, but he did not dare let her go out of his arms.

"You can smile," she joked.

He exhaled and kissed her on the forehead.

"Well, Troy and I were about to make love and you sent a text and I couldn't go through with it. And I just knew then that my world would never be the same."

"Oh, Elisa, you just don't know what you are doing to me at this moment. If I die right now—"tears began to form in his eyes—"Ms. Martin, this would be enough for me to go to heaven and be contented. My soul is at peace right now! I love you, Elisa Martin. Will you accompany me to Paris for at least two weeks? At least until I can decide what our next move is?"

Elisa paused, and she blushed. Her eyes were already light brown they looked like glass. She could not believe what she was hearing, and she was ready to go with him. She stared off and she didn't answer him right away, so it made him panic.

"I'm sorry. I didn't mean to move so fast! Please forgive me, baby?"

Baby, she said in her head. *This man is really trying to kill me now*. She was admiring him so much she couldn't say a word. "Um, no, no, I'm not being rushed at all. In fact, Rhonda and I are planning a trip as we speak to come and meet you and tell you how much I love you."

They both busted out into laughter. They realized that she was talking as if he wasn't the one she was going to see.

"Elisa, I'm here. You already told me, so do you still want to go with me? I will love showing you Paris and showing you off to all my friends, especially Sam. He is my best friend, and he knows how much I love you."

CAN'T STOP DESTINY

"Oh my god, I forgot. What about Molina? She is going to think we planned all of this. I really like her, William! I really care about her feelings!"

"I care about her too, baby. She is a remarkable woman. She reminded me so much of you I almost went further with our relationship. But I realized it was you I want, and that would not be fair to her. So when she came over last night, and Rhonda was telling me about how you feel about me, I panicked, and I hurt her feelings."

"Wait, Rhonda! Rhonda was there last night? She was the other woman you were talking to?"

"Yes, she came over last night and told me she was looking for me because she knew how you felt about me, and she was tired of seeing her best friend suffering."

"Oh no, no, she didn't. Oh my god, that is why I love her so much. We were at the beach yesterday, and she made me turn around so she could find a store—that suddenly disappeared." Elisa started laughing, with tears of joy mixed with it.

"Yes, she found it all right. She parked in front of my home and Sam found her. We invited her in, and one thing led to another. Molina came, confessing her feelings for me, and I had to tell her that I love another woman, which was you, love."

She pulled him close to her, and she kissed him like he was already hers. "I love you, William Harris. I will always love you forever."

They held each other so tightly. Everyone left the office as they realized this was not just another man but someone special. Elisa and William went to her private room at her business. He held her, and they fell asleep together all night long.

CHAPTER 20

The sun was shining bright, and it was six thirty in the morning. William had already left and went in the break room to make coffee. He noticed some Community coffee, a lot of it. It was his favorite, and as he looked, he said to himself, *Apparently, she loves it also.*

As Elisa turned over, she felt like she had been dreaming, but she noticed a pair of men's shoes by her bed, and she began to blush. She jumped up, ran to the bathroom, and brushed her teeth.

Man, I'm glad I let Rhonda convince me to put a toothbrush in here. She thought back to when she bought it.

"Okay, Elisa, you might have a man over, so you need to keep toothbrushes in your office, not just a bed, ma'am," Rhonda joked.

"No, ma'am, I don't need a toothbrush," Elisa said in a serious tone. "I don't plan on doing anything here but working and resting on my long days. Thank you, ma'am!"

"Yes, yes, um, here, put it in the basket for a rainy day." Rhonda gave her that look. "Party pooper," she said under her breath.

"I heard that," Elisa said, smiling as she paid for all the items.

CAN'T STOP DESTINY

Elisa brushed her teeth, and as she was about to go into the break room, she realized someone was bringing her some coffee. She could smell it down the hall.

"It is kind of early for Tricia to be making coffee. Oh no, Tricia. I hope she didn't see William leaving out of here!"

As Elisa went to see if he left her a message, he walked in the office without a shirt on and two cups of coffee. She almost passed out from looking at his gorgeous body and her favorite coffee in his hands. He blushed, and she walked toward him.

"Good morning, baby. Here is some coffee, and it's my favorite. I see good minds think alike?"

"Yes, we do, William," she said, smiling. "Good morning, and yes, that's my favorite also, and one cup will do me through, and I usually rewarm it all day. That is why my cup is so big." She laughed and took her cup. As she reached for it, he pulled her close to him.

"Did I tell you I love you, Elisa?"

"I love you too, Will, always."

As they finished the coffee, he got into his shoes and washed up. And as he walked out the bathroom, she grabbed his hand and put something in it.

"What's this, love?"

"My numbers. Use them soon."

"I will be because I plan on getting our plane tickets today, and you need to be packed and ready ASAP, lady. I'm not letting you change your mind on me. You forgot I know how driven you are. I can't let you out of my vision yet."

"I haven't changed my mind, but it's something I didn't tell you. I invited Rhonda to go with me before we planned to be together. And she did put us together."

"You are right, Elisa, and she deserves a free trip for bringing my wife back into my life."

Elisa just paused and stared at him. He said *wife*, and she didn't know how to take it.

"Elisa, I meant just what I said." He kissed her and walked off.

She was so stunned she barely said bye.

157

As she went into the closet to get dressed before someone did catch her in the act of doing nothing, she smiled. She decided to put on her designer suit. She had a few appointments she needed to take care of, and as she was walking out of the office, Tricia walked in as the phone was ringing.

"Good morning, Ms. Elisa. I see you made the coffee this morning. I could smell it down the hall."

"Thank you. It's the least I could do for one of the best assistants on this side of Pensacola."

She walked off smiling so hard Tricia stared, smiling, trying to say thank you while answering the phone.

"Hello, hello," she said in her shock. "Good morning, this is Family Therapy Clinic. How can I help you, Tricia speaking?" She was happy to be considered a good assistant.

"Hi, this is William. I am calling to confirm a lunch date with Ms. Martin."

"Um, let me see, sir." Tricia looked into her organizer for the week. "Excuse me, sir. William, is it?"

"Yes, ma'am."

"Sir, I don't seem to have you down for a lunch date for today. I apologize for this oversight. But if you need me to, I can talk to Ms. Martin and reschedule the luncheon for a more convenient time."

"Ma'am, I'm sure she will want this date. Can you confirm 12:30 p.m. today for me?" William said, smiling on the other side of the phone. He felt seventeen again. He didn't know how to act or how fast or slow to move. He just knew he was not going to let her out of his life or sight again anytime soon.

"Hold on, sir, while I confirm. Thank you."

Tricia noticed that she was not in her office, so she called her on her cell.

"Ms. Elisa, you have a gentleman that is calling to confirm a luncheon for 12:30 today. I apologize I did not set the date, but he was persistent."

"Um, well, I didn't plan any date, and what is his name, Tricia?" she said as she was dipping her doughnut in her coffee.

"It's Mr. William, ma'am."

"Oh, oh yes, please confirm that it is a date, and let me know what he says."

Elisa started to blush. She almost skipped down the hall if it didn't look bad for a psychologist doctor to be doing that in front of people that she helped with mental problems.

"Mr. William," she said, "it is confirmed, and is there anything else she will need to do for the luncheon? Will she have to meet you somewhere so I can have her driver bring her?"

"*No!*" he said, excited. "I will pick her up around 12:30. Tell her thanks and dito."

"Ditto." Tricia blushed, and she was wondering, *Has this anything to do with the Romeo that was in her office last night?*

As Elisa walked back, she smiled at everyone in the office, her customers and Tricia. As she passed by her, she said, "You can send my first patient in, Ms. Tricia." She was smiling harder than normal.

"Yes, ma'am, I will."

As some of the patients walked in, Molina walked in. She was noticing the morning rush—kids everywhere, parents telling their children to mind, teenagers slouched down in their seats because they didn't want to be, quote on quote, seeing a crazy doctor.

"Good morning, Tricia. Did Elisa have anything specific for me to do today? I know I have one client, and she asked me to take any walk-ins. But if you need me, I am in my office. I'm going to get me some coffee. Had a late night."

"Really?" Tricia blushed. "So what's up with you and Elisa and your late nights? She even has a lunch date."

"Really?" Molina smiled. "Time she lives a little. So do tell. Who is this man sent from heaven?"

"Well, I can tell you this. I wanted him to be my children's father, but apparently, he was spoken for Ms. Martin. He came in yesterday, walking in here with his humble smile and good looks. Molina, he is so gorgeous. But when she saw him, she rushed to her office. She did not want to see him. Before we knew it, everyone, including the patients, could hear him and her hollering and how very upset she was with him. But whatever the god said made her smile turn up, and she is in such good spirits."

As they were talking, Molina noticed her appointment come in. "We will talk later. I have to congratulate her but later. Thanks, Tricia, for the info."

As time went by, it was almost time for William to go get Elisa. He had to call Rhonda and tell her the good news on his way to go pick her up.

"Hello, Mr. Harris. Do I hear smiles through the phone?"

"Hello, Rhonda. I hadn't talked to you yet."

"I know, but Elisa texted me, and she couldn't tell me everything, but she did say she is on cloud nine, thanks to Mr. William Harris."

"She said that, Rhonda? I make her float?"

"Oh my god, you both are so out of here. Do tell, Will."

"Well, long story short, that is my wife. She is going to Paris with me this week, and because you brought us back together, your trip is paid in full. I've already booked the flight. Sam and I are packing as we speak."

"Really!" Rhonda said as she was screaming. "Thank you so much, William. I really don't know what to say. I just know that I had to help fate bring my best friend and her long-lost love back together."

"Rhonda, she is a breath of fresh air. She is everything I imagine her to be. She still looks like that seventeen-year-old girl, and I feel like that also. I hurt for years, but it was worth the pain just to see that she loves me as much as I love her."

"I'm so happy for the both of you, and I have a lot of planning to do ASAP."

"Yes, ASAP because I have so much planned for you both. I'm on my way to her office. We have a luncheon date so I can tell her everything is in the making."

"Hey, what about Molina? You forgot she works there."

"Oh no! I clearly forgot, but she must face this one day. I can't keep hiding behind her pain. I do care, but, Rhonda, I waited so long." William got quiet. He didn't want to hurt Molina, no more than she had already been hurt, but he had to let fate do what it does. "Well, Rhonda, I made it to her office which, by the way, is immaculate. I'm so proud of her. She is so unique and smart, and—"

CAN'T STOP DESTINY

"Hey, I'm starting to get jealous. Why can't a man say that about me?"

"Rhonda, keep living. You will hear that and more. You are a remarkable woman. I knew that when you were my student and when you walked into my house the other night. That is why I pushed you so hard."

"Really? I thought it was because you wanted Elisa to wait for me every other day while I was in tutorials so you can look at her."

"Oh my god, did you think of me like that all those years ago?"

"Yes, everybody but you two knew that you care about each other."

William smiled and parked his Porsche as close to her front door as he could get. As he walked out, he told Rhonda goodbye.

"Goodbye, William. Take it easy on Molina. I saw how desperate you get about Elisa."

"Okay," he said as he blushed and hung up the phone.

As he walked into the practice, he saw Tricia, and he flagged her to him.

"Hi, Mr. William. Why are you hiding back here?"

"Good day. Can you tell Elisa to meet me in the break room, please?"

"Yes, sir," she said. As she went into Elisa's office, she was deep into a session.

"Excuse me, Ms. Martin, but someone is here to see you and asks that you meet them in the break room," Tricia said, blushing, making Elisa know it was William.

"Um, excuse me. I will be right back," she told her patient.

"Why does he want me to meet him in the break room? I'm almost through, you could have told him."

"Well, he looked quite desperate."

Elisa started getting butterflies; she hadn't felt that since the last time they talked. *What could be the problem? Had he changed his mind?* she was wondering.

"Hi, Will," she said as she walked in slow. William took her hand and pulled her closer to him. As he kissed her, she could feel him deep in her soul.

161

"Baby, we have a slight problem, and I need your help in handling it."

"Um, yes, William? What is it?"

"Baby, I'm here in your office, and I did it on purpose."

"What? Um, Will, you are confusing me for real."

"Baby, we have to face Molina together."

"Oh no, I forgot she works here. I forgot all about you guys' relationship!"

"Hey, baby, wait, wait. It wasn't a relationship. It was just what it was. She made it more than I planned for it to be."

"Sure, Mr. Harris. I'm just, um, the girl that waited her whole young adult life for you. You have a way that makes women crazy!"

He smiled as he looked into her eyes. He stared so hard and so long all she could do was stare back and put her head down.

"No, ma'am," he said as he raised her head. "I love you, Elisa Martin. Get used to these stares. I want you to feel me when you can't hear me. I can't breathe without you, Elisa."

He held her so close, and he kissed her so hard they were bumping teeth. As they were kissing, Molina walked in to get some more coffee.

As they were kissing, she began to blush.

"Ahem," she said. "You have a guest, Ms. Martin."

As Elisa let go of William, they looked into each other's eyes as if to say "oh no, now what!" Molina looked at her, and seeing who he was, she felt as if she was going to die.

"Elisa, how could you? William, how could you!" she said, stunned.

"Wait, Molina, we can explain it all. Please do not leave," they both asked her at the same time.

"Why!" Molina yelled, making everyone in the office look toward the break room. "Why should I stay here and watch the two people I trusted be in each other arms? Elisa, I trusted you. I told you all about William, and you betrayed me like this."

She burst into tears, and William walked over to her to comfort her.

"Please hear us out, Molina, please?" William said as Elisa stared out of shock and hurt for her employee.

CAN'T STOP DESTINY

"What, William? What can you say to explain how you to betrayed me! Elisa," she said in whisper as she barely could talk. "Why?"

Elisa fell into tears for her hurt, and she didn't know where to start.

"Molina, when you first came to me about William, I knew it was my William, but I hadn't seen Will in years. And I chose to hurt and let you both be happy."

"Happy? How could we be happy? He wouldn't give me a chance after he treated me like only any woman with good sense would want to feel. He decided that he wanted to be my friend and that he was in love with someone else. Oh no, please tell me, Elisa, it wasn't you!"

"Yes, Molina, it was her." William spoke up for her. "But you don't understand. The night I met you, I had met so many women before you. But you were the one woman that came close to making me feel what I feel for Elisa. Molina, I saw all what I loved about Elisa in you. I didn't want to hurt you, so I pulled back until I could figure out what to do. And just as I was about to give up on Elisa and I, her friend came over that night and told me Elisa was upset because she was in love with me and that she thought she had lost me to you, not realizing that I still loved her too. For years, Molina, I tried to go forward. I just couldn't. And I didn't plan to hurt you, but I couldn't replace what I feel with hurting you. I promise this is all true! You are a remarkable woman, and some man is going to be blessed to have you. But Molina, I'm in love with Elisa, have been for six years."

They all got quiet.

"Elisa, is this true? Please tell me you did not plan to come between William and I?"

Elisa cried and walked over to Molina and grabbed her hands.

"Molina, I really wanted to let it be and allow you guys to pursue what future you could have. I promise William came to me when I was still hurting for you and not knowing the woman you were talking about in his heart was me."

Molina walked off to the window. She got quiet and stared out. Elisa and William looked hopeless, caring for her and not knowing what to do next.

163

"Oh my god, all this time you must have been hurting so badly. You care that much, Elisa, you would give up William Harris of all people."

Molina turned to William, looking at him. "William, you are such a remarkable man. Any woman would fall for you. I'm so sorry we all had to go through such hurt. But I need some time to adjust to all of this. But, Ms. Elisa, I believe you. You have always been true with me." She hugged Elisa and walked out of the break room as everyone was staring. She looked at Tricia and said, "I will be back. I'm going on my break. Can you handle things until I return?"

"Yes, ma'am, Ms. Molina," she said, confused about all the yelling she heard. *What can I do to comfort her?* Tricia asked herself. They both were her friends, and one was her boss. She walked to her desk and called the next doctor on duty to assist Molina with her next patient. As Molina drove off, Elisa could see her from the break room. She hugged William tightly and started to cry.

"I'm so sorry she had to be in the middle of this. It wasn't in the plan to get you back, but it sure feels like it."

"Elisa, it was in the plan. It was God's plan, and we have to trust he is in everything. I'm sorry she was hurt, but I can't lose you to what could have been. You are my air, woman."

They kissed and held each other for a long time.

CHAPTER 21

"If I have to remember one more thing, I will throw all these clothes out of this suitcase and forget this much-needed trip. I can't believe I trusted my employees to handle my affairs with my dream business just taking off. But God knows, if I don't take a vacation, I won't have a business because I won't be here to have it. She laughed hysterically, falling back on the bed. She was so happy to finally be away from it all. And leaving with William did not make it any harder for her to leave. She grabbed her Burberry luggage and her designer outfits. She did her final packing and zipped up her luggage. As she was packing, she heard the doorbell ring.

"Who could that be at a time like this? I already have rocks in my stomach. Feels like some kind of dream you didn't imagine but is happening."

"Hello," she said as she walked down the hall to her front door. "Hello," she said again as she peeped through the door window.

"Hello," the voice said on the other side. "I have a delivery for Ms. Martin. Elisa Martin, ma'am."

As she opened the door, a gentleman gave her something to sign as another man walked in with a dozen red roses, dozens of yellow roses, and Turtle's candy, which is her favorite, and a card with a message.

"Have a good evening, ma'am."

"Wait, sirs, just a minute."

165

PAMELA GREEN

Elisa walked into her kitchen in her stash spot where she kept money for pizza and any other kind of delivery when she was going to have a long night doing updates. As she gave each gentleman ten dollars each, they smiled, and she couldn't wait to close the door and read the note.

> Hello, baby. The red roses are to let you know I still love you, always, and the yellow roses is to let you know I'm glad I have my friend again and, hopefully, for life. I will be sending a driver to get you in about thirty minutes. If you aren't ready, I will be there in five minutes anyway.
>
> Love you,
> William, *Always*

Elisa screamed, smelled the roses, grabbed her candy and started eating them.

I can't believe he remembered my favorite candy. I remember the late nights helping him on his testing and setting up his plans for the week, how he would ask what I wanted from the store. She was rethinking it all, and it made her blush so hard. As she was chewing and blushing, the phone rang.

Oh no, he said thirty minutes. Who could this be? She didn't want to answer.

"Hello," she said anxiously.

"Hi, my lovely daughter, the love of my life!"

"Mother, is this you? And hi to you too, the love of my life also."

"So are you all ready for your big trip?"

"Almost, Mother. He'll be here in a few. I just need to make sure I have everything. Mother, you'll never guess what he did."

"I can imagine. He has always charmed you off your feet without trying."

"Mother, he gave me roses, red for love and yellow for friendship. And to top that, Mom, he remembered my favorite candy."

"No, he did not. Turtle's!"

166

CAN'T STOP DESTINY

"Yes, Momma. He remembers my Turtle's." She felt like crying.

"Oh my god, I'm so happy for my little girl. Elisa, you deserve him, baby. It's been a long time coming. God heard your prayers, and he saw your suffering. It's your time."

"You think, Mom, you think?" she said, barely able to talk for wanting to cry but fighting it.

"Yes, my child. It is real. God doesn't make mistakes. I just hope you can wait to make me a grandmother."

"Mother, I'm going to wait. I've waited this long, and I'm sure he wants it that way, at least I hope." She paused and wondered, *Could he wait a little longer?* "I didn't think of that, Mother!" she said slowly.

"Elisa, he will, if that's what you want as a gift to him on your wedding night. If he is the one, he will wait. Elisa, he is the one. I'm pretty sure of it."

"Mother, is it fair to make him wait after the many years we've been separated? I know he is experienced than I am."

"Let fate do what it does. Just know if you don't, don't condemn yourself. Repent, pick up, and try again. That is why God sent his Son. Remember what we raised you to believe, and that God is not a God of bondage, but he is a God of love and justice, meaning, baby, don't make it happen. Let it happen, okay?"

"Thank you, Mom. You always know what to say and when to say it. I don't know if I told you this, but you are my best friend, not just my mother."

There was silence on the phone.

"Mother?"

"Yes, Elisa," her mother said with tears on the other end of the phone.

"Mommy, all those years being with you and watching you protecting me and Stan Junior and loving all those patients and loving Dad enough not to kill him when he gave you twin boys"—they both busted out into laughter—"Mommy, that is why I love you. And I've never felt like you were overprotective because you made room for failure, and you gave us a life most people dream of, the finer things of life. But I call you my friend because you have always told me like

I needed it, and you didn't let things, jobs, or people separate you from us. I love you, Mom. I hope I've made you proud of me."

"You have, my baby, and keep up the hard work. Life is just starting, believe me. Enjoy your youth and William. He is a good catch, straight from heaven."

"Thank you so much, Mom."

As Elisa's tears were about to build up, the doorbell rang.

"Ma, I think it's William. I will call you when we arrive, and kiss Dad for me and the twins. I will call Stan Junior also when I arrive, or he will kill me."

"Goodbye, precious, and have a great trip."

She ran down the hall to make sure she was looking up to part. She ran back, out of breath, and said, "Just a moment please."

As she peeped through the door, she felt like she couldn't breathe. There he was, standing, looking amazing. He was dressed in a designer outfit, and he was wearing it well. He knocked again.

"Hello, Elisa. It's been thirty minutes. I hope you are not reneging on me?"

"No," she said as she opened the door. She was smiling so hard she knew her face was stuck to the back of her face.

"Hi, love," he said as he walked in, hugging her. "Elisa." He looked into her eyes.

"Yes, William?" she said softly.

"Lady of my life, I don't know how to put it into words. You are everything to me now and always have been. What I'm trying to say is I love you, and I hope you really feel the same."

"Yes, William, I feel the same, and you have been my everything since you walked into my life six years ago."

William went into his back pocket, and as he pulled out a small velvet box, he went on his knees. "Elisa," he said looking into her eyes.

"William," she said, about to lose her breathe.

"Elisa, I know it's you I want forever. I've been all over the world. I've met so many ladies in different languages, shapes, colors. Elisa, none of them could compare to you. None of them had the power to do for me what you did in just a glimpse of you. Elisa, my love, my

CAN'T STOP DESTINY

life, and my heart, I will die without you. You are the air I breathe. Please make me a happy man and be my wife until death we do part."

She looked at him looking up at her. She could not believe he was proposing to her, and she did not believe what she was about to tell him.

"William, all the years I waited for you, all the fears of losing you to another woman because of my age, and the days I worked harder and stronger to forget you—you walked into my life just when I needed you the most. I have a career that I love. I've finished college because you made me a good student. I've even invested in my own home. But none of that fulfilled me until you walked into my office. I knew then that I had not breathed until I exhaled that day you walked into my office. Yes, William, I will marry you, and I will love you and have your children, and I will be the wife you need until death do we part."

He pulled out a round-cut 18-karat solitaire diamond white-gold ring. It was so beautiful, and he put it on her finger. As he was about to get up, she kneeled to him. And she held him, and they both exhaled.

"William, baby?" she said as he kissed her forehead.

"Yes, my love?" he whispered.

"Baby, I guess you *can't stop destiny*."

There is more to come with the next book
in the series, *Can't Stop Destiny 2!*